To Lindsay

All the best
Jim

At night the rules changed.

Normality determined that most locked themselves away. They turned a blind-eye against the things happening outside their front door.

And that was the time that the lawless slipped out to prey on the vulnerable.

2022

Other Books by Jim Ody

Lost Connections
The Place That Never Existed
A Cold Retreat
Beneath The Whispers
…Just South of Heaven
Noah's Lament
Mr Watcher
The Revenge of Lisa Lipstick
Mystery Island
Tales From The Coffee Pot

<u>Hudson Bell Series:</u>
A Lifetime Ago
Come Back Home

<u>Tall Trees Series:</u>
Little Miss Evil

<u>Joel Baxter Series</u>
The Crazy Season

<u>Question Mark Horror Series:</u>
Camp Death

Sweet Vigilante

?

Question Mark Press

Jim Ody

All rights reserved. No part of this publication may be reproduced, distributed or transmitted in any form or by any means, without prior written permission.

First published in 2021 by Question Mark Press

Copyright © 2021 by Jim Ody

?

Question Mark Press

This is a work of fiction. Names, characters, places, and incidents are a product of the author's imagination. Locales and public names are sometimes used for atmospheric purposes. Any resemblance to actual people, living or dead, or to businesses, companies, events, institutions, or locales is completely coincidental.

Sweet Vigilante/ Jim Ody. – 1st edition
ISBN: 9798491967865
Cover design by: Elli Toney
Blog Tours by: Zooloo's Book Tours

Part 1

# Prologue

Perplexed, the unwanted child sat in the back seat of the car. The world sped by with irrelevance; a blur of shapes and colours that meant nothing to her. A one-way journey that would shape her life forever.

She'd been fiddling with a paperclip in her fingers throughout. Busy fingers to help her anxiety. She carefully placed the object onto her leg and stared at it. With a gritted-teeth determination, all of her focus was channelled to the inanimate object.

Her hands were placed on the seat beside her, the paperclip wobbled. It might've been a bump in the road or the reverberations from the vehicle's gruff engine. It might have been anything.

Slowly, and without explanation, the paperclip wiggled and then moved. Not left or right, but vertically lifting a few millimetres off her leg.

She smiled and let out her breath as it suddenly dropped hitting her leg before bouncing off onto the floor.

She rested back in her seat and concluded that despite it all this might be the best thing in the world.

Jim Ody

Outside, pregnant thunderclouds hunched together plotting some meteorological doom. They frowned over the vehicle as it headed down unfamiliar winding roads. Knowing eyes from above narrowed. But unknown forces could only do so much.

The expensive and large black German car crunched over some sporadic piles of gravel and pulled to a standstill outside the house. The track was muddy, and the grass strewn with children's abandoned toys. Once brightly coloured, the array of plastic was now dull and broken—the perfect analogy for the children themselves. Jagged edges pleaded for an opportunity to scratch upon innocent skin. An old swing creaked in pain as the wind antagonised it. The seat was no longer level. Hidden in the long grass were sharp shards of glass. Evidence of violence from a time forgotten. Things had got out of hand.

The house was large and domineering. The dark brickwork was covered in ivy that held together the secrets from within. It was doing its best to muffle the screams, and cries for help, tightening its grip and strangling the lives within.

Set miles away from the city limits, it was eerie and quiet. Screams would go unnoticed, and children could disappear without a trace. If nobody admitted you were missing, then who would ever know?

A foreigner to these parts, the lady got out of the car. She struggled to suppress her disdain at a residence that didn't care for appearances. It was a world which she couldn't comprehend. Nevertheless, she smoothed her skirt and looked from her immaculate heels to the dirty puddles goading her all the way to the house. Her freshly painted lips curled slightly at the hovel that this place represented. She couldn't stand to be here any longer than was necessary. It made her nauseous. The Eggs Benedict she'd enjoyed for her breakfast now sat uneasy in her stomach.

"Get out," she demanded, her face stern and her voice harsh. The child cowered in the back. Her arms wrapped around her toy bunny for some comfort. The little girl hoped it was a mistake. Whatever it was she'd done wrong, she'd never do again. Her mind raced at what that could've been, but she knew anything and everything seemed to set her mother off.

"If I have to drag you out, I will!" The woman hissed through perfect white teeth. She didn't need this. She had a lot to get done, and this selfish snivelling child was, as usual, getting in the way.

The child reluctantly shifted over the seat. Still clutching her bunny, her arm was grabbed painfully by the woman. "Now!"

The soft eyes and slight curl in the girl's blonde hair would've been enough to melt the hearts of anyone. But the relationship of mother and daughter was a bondless charade on the part of the mother and unrequited love from the child. The only thing the child represented was a heavy burden stopping her from getting to where she needed to be in life. The woman sometimes found it hard to believe she'd spawned the child and rued the day she drank too much Champagne and threw up the protection of her contraception pill over the lap of the business man, who would quickly impregnate her and disappear. By the time she realised she was carrying, she was too far

Jim Ody

gone. She could do nothing but go through with the disgusting ordeal, whilst she watched her peers push her to the corporate floor as they continued to climb the ladder of success. But this was her time now, and she'd be damned if this little bitch was going to stop her.

She cleared her throat, and hoped she looked the part of a grieving woman, struggling with such a heartbreaking decision. Of course, she'd been looking forward to this day for weeks. Probably months, or years, but they didn't need to know that. She badly wanted to glance at her watch, but couldn't break character. This was taking so much damn time!

There was movement from inside the house. They had been expected.

A man and woman were full of smiles. They'd made an effort, but the mother still saw the uncouth underlying appearance of the lower-class. You can only dress shit up so much. As they walked up to the couple, she began to wonder what they were so happy about. They already had a brood and were willing to take on this ungrateful brat at the drop of a hat. Maybe they were on drugs.

"Hello, there!" the man grinned. He was large and smartly dressed. Hair freshly combed and smelling like he'd bathed in Old Spice. The woman was smaller, and her face looked guarded, even behind a smile. She was rotund, and wearing a blouse over charcoal grey leggings. At one time she might've looked cute. She had large lips, but it was clear cigarettes had dried out her skin, darkened her teeth, and aged her considerably. She'd done her best to look presentable, but she wouldn't be on a magazine cover any time soon.

"Hi," the mother said, thrusting the child in front of her. "This is Gina."

The other woman stepped forward from the man, and held out her arms, as if ready to accept the gift. The child looked up at the woman she knew to be her mother, unsure what was going on. Her eyes pleaded to go home. Back to her friends. Back to the life she'd always known. The one she'd woken up to that morning and thought it to be that way forever.

Instead, her mother pushed her towards the outstretched arms of the stranger. The man looked at her like she was something exciting. His eyes grew wide. He was struggling to hide his pleasure.

There it was. Blink and you'd miss it. The man's tongue shot out to his lips and back in again. A snake, smelling the air. Tasting the scent of his new prey.

"She's all yours," the mother said devoid of emotion whilst handing over an envelope thick with cash. The sentence and actions carried more repercussions than anyone would realise.

"Thank you," the man said, nodding and swallowing hard. "We'll take good care of her." It was words of expectation and duty muttered without conviction. The kid was of no concern to her anymore.

The mother shrugged, and with nothing more to say, turned her back and walked away. The man inside the car didn't even look out, instead started up the engine, and before Gina could look at them, they were gone. And she was left crying for a mother who had just thrown her to the lions.

Jim Ody

"Come on, dear," the woman said, holding her hand. Her grip was tight. Too tight. Her small fingers hurt.

Their pace was quick as they got to the house. She was virtually dragging her to the door. They opened it and pushed her inside. She stopped crying to take in the dark and dirty surroundings.

"What's your name, pretty?" the man said, but the kindness had gone. He removed his shirt to reveal a dirty vest. It was smeared and ripped. Some of it looked like ketchup, but mostly it looked like blood.

"Gina," she said in a frightened voice.

He nodded. "Well, Gina, the fun times are over. I'm the boss. You'll do as I say or you will die. Understand?"

She couldn't believe the words. She felt so scared and so alone. She hugged her bunny and began to cry.

"Tears are a sign of disobedience. The more you cry, the more you will hurt. A child can only take so much pain." His eyes narrowed, and he raised a hand in threat.

She sniffed back the tears instead and tried not to blubber. It was hard. Probably the hardest thing she'd ever had to do.

"You're probably not going to like it here too much. D'you know what? I don't care." He looked amused, but each word was spat with contempt.

From there he was true to his word. She didn't like it there very much, and he certainly didn't care about her or the other children. Feeling pain and hiding your feelings was something she'd learn to cope with.

She now understood what Hell on Earth might be like.

Chapter One

Many years later.

The smell of rain hung in the atmosphere; the showers had been chased out of town by the winds. Large clouds were now camouflaged by the cloak of darkness. The night lights took over the city. Danger slunk out in the shadows, baring its teeth and licking its lips with anticipation. The flashing neon glow of signs was designed to pull in the punters with offers of cheap entertainment.

She sat up high above the buildings. The proof of rain still evident across the intricate expanse of roof-works. The busy pipework of air conditioning hidden from below.

She surveyed her city. That was how she saw it. Not because she held any power – she was a nobody – but because she had an uncontrollable urge to help others. It was clichéd, but she wanted to make the world a better place.

Sweet Vigilante

A thankless task. An impossible task. But each journey starts with a few small steps. And without optimism, there would be no reason to go on.

Throughout the day, the city was a hustle and bustle of people busy with their complex lives. For the most part, they are too caught up with themselves to care about others. All around were eyes and ears, cameras and phones capturing it all. The police, even at capacity, could barely cope with most daylight crime. There was a safety-in-numbers mentality that almost eradicated any irrelevant fears.

But at night the rules changed. Normality determined that most locked themselves away. They turned a blind-eye against the things happening outside their front door. And that was the time that the lawless slipped out to prey on the vulnerable.

This wasn't the early evening where youngsters and partygoers spilled into the streets looking for alcohol and new acquaintances. No, this was later on. A little past midnight when most people had found their way either into their own bed, or into someone else's. That was when evil appeared.

She moved with silence down the external emergency staircase. She was open to the elements outside but fully focused on the scene below.

A lone woman had decided to take the infamous shortcut between the two buildings. A rash and flippant roll of the dice stacked high with risk. Ignoring the advice from others, she'd had a senseless disregard for their pessimistic tales. To her they were one-in-a-million chances and likened it to being hit by a plane falling out of the sky.

Jim Ody

Like rats sniffing the air, two chancer lads stepped out of the darkness. A flash of light showed grins slapped on their faces; they couldn't believe their luck. Dressed in dark hoodies and of medium and average height and size, they were carefree in their actions. What did it matter? If they were seen no one would be able to pick them out in a line up. They looked like every other cocky teenager walking around with a swagger wearing oversized jogging-bottoms at half-mast, proudly showing off their designer smalls to all around.

The girl had her mobile in her hand like a threat. They laughed as she held it as a weapon.

"What ya' gonna do with that, sweetheart?" the adolescent voice barked out from the hood. He was enjoying the power he had.

"Maybe she wants a snap of my cock?" the other one added. They both laughed at that.

Watching the scene unfold, the woman from above stepped down into the alley and like a cat moved out behind the girl.

The first guy noticed her straight away. He opened up his arms like he was showing how much bigger he was.

"Uh-oh, what have we got here? Looks like we both get one now, eh?"

The scared girl whipped her head around, assuming the worst. She tried to smile as she saw the woman with bright red hair but was too scared to fully commit. She regretted her decision on the detour and fear held her rigid to the spot.

Sweet Vigilante

"You boys lost?" the woman asked in a low confident voice.

"Lost?" the talker said, slapping his friend on the back. "Seems to me I just found God. How 'bout you perform something for me? Take me ta heaven, init?"

With more feline movements, the woman glided past the girl and confronted the boys. "How about you turn around and go home? Do that, and I'll let you walk."

"I like a feisty woman!" he said, still full of piss and vinegar. He acted like he was intoxicated, but actually he was clean and sober. This was just the evil he'd been brought up on.

"Seriously. Go home, and we'll forget about it, right?" Her voice still remained even. Unlike a man she didn't feel the need to puff out her chest or shout out obscenities.

The girl looked more scared but managed to stumble backwards a couple of steps. Each one towards potential freedom.

"Fuck you, love!" Big gob said and walked forward. His hands now clenched as tightly as his jaw. An animal looking to attack.

"Stay back!" she said, but it was too late. In one swift move he pulled out a knife and leaped at her.

She hated knives. They were unpredictable and never easy to defend. One slight miscalculation could be fatal. A blade had no conscience, it sliced through whatever was in its path and needed little force to cause irreversible damage.

The guy was experienced at holding a knife but clearly not at using one. He lunged with his arm outstretched and wrist turned downwards. She grabbed the wrist and allowed it to go past her, as she used her other hand to chop up against his elbow. It was a painful move. Not enough to break bones but enough for the knife to drop from his hand.

Her knee thrust up into his genitals. As he dropped, she kicked her other knee into his jaw like an uppercut, and he folded to the floor.

The other lad came at her, but for him it was out of duty and not for a love of violence. He hadn't been confident to start with. He wasn't a fighter. He swung his arms high and wide like a drunk. They were the sort of punches you could see the minute he thought about throwing them. She easily bobbed and weaved, allowing him to have a go. But with each punch thrown that missed, his energy soon was spent.

She flicked out a double jab straight down the middle and made direct contact with his nose. That was enough. The jab is one of the most important punches in boxing and for good reason. It sends a spike of pain and also stops your opponent from swinging back. He stopped, held up his hands, took one look at his mate moaning on the ground, and ran off as fast as he could.

"Come on," the woman said to the girl. The girl nodded and silently followed her.

"This place isn't good for a girl like you. I don't mean any disrespect, but the night is crawling with these lowlifes. They'll prey on you without thought."

"Thank you," the girl said. "I owe you."

"You don't owe me a thing. You owe yourself to stay out of trouble."

"I know."

Sweet Vigilante

"Now let's get you safely home."

That's what she did. She looked out for the weak and the needy. Who else was going to help them?

She was a good Samaritan with a kick-arse attitude.

She was a vigilante of the night.

Chapter Two

A glass smashed in the kitchen. It's sound loud against the silent backdrop of a lazy Sunday afternoon in the flat. She was already panicking. The destructive sound was enough to cause psychological pain. Fear from her youth.

"Pops!" Gina shouted as she leapt up, threw her paperback down, and ran towards where she'd heard the noise.

The old man was sitting on the floor, holding his chest with his right hand, and looking bewildered and confused. His eyes darted around the room, and he looked troubled and unable to focus. A mass of broken glass surrounded him. Fear gripped her.

"You okay?" she asked in panicked tones, reaching down and slipping an arm around him. His silence was a sure sign that he was anything but okay. "Be careful."

Pops nodded and accepted her help. "Just a spell," he said. "I'm okay now." Always the hero, he refused to accept that he was getting old.

"Like hell you are. Sit down here," she said, guiding him to the chair and rang for an ambulance. She tried to remain calm and not panic. Her pulse raced and her stomach sank to the floor. Her heart beat hard for this old guy. He was everything to her.

"Don't go bothering nobod," he said in the way he always did. It was a mock irritation even if deep down she suspected he enjoyed the fuss. He was an old-school independent man in his seventies who had worked hard and fought harder for everything his whole life. But of late, he had started to show signs that time was catching up with him, and he was no longer able to outrun it. He was resigned to the sudden realisation he was mortal and started to grudgingly accept help.

"You need checking over," she said to him. "You're not young anymore!" She tried to inject some humour into it, but both knew she was right.

"Ain't no need for no fuss," he mumbled, though complying. He was a lot of things but a fool he wasn't. He'd fight, but in the end he'd do what she said. Their mutual respect was strong and true.

"We'll see," she replied with a half-smile. Inside her heart continued to pound. She was worried about the old man. He had been the only person in her life that had ever cared about her. If something happened to him then she didn't know what she'd do.

Pops was silent when the ambulance arrived, not half as talkative as he normally was. His jokes had taken a sabbatical – another sign that things were serious. They wheeled him off, and in a slight panic Gina followed behind.

His frail hand fumbled with the oxygen mask as he wheezed out, "Tell Lynne." He got a stern warning from the paramedic, but Gina shouted that she would.

Lynne was a close friend of Pops who lived in the same building. They acted like a married couple who loved each other but lived separately. She was an author who stayed up most of the night writing. She had published over one hundred books and saw no reason to stop any time soon. Her book covers bore her pen-name of Olivier DePrux, and the name certainly fit her better. There was something continental about her. Perhaps it was her elegant dress, or how she had aged so well. You had to look twice to confirm her to not be a youngster in her forties.

Her hair was in a grown-out bob, and her voice was gravelly through a lifetime of cigarettes. Gina didn't know much about her leg, other than it was no longer attached to her body. The prosthetic replacement could be slightly cumbersome compared to a normal appendage, but she never talked about it. Just moved in a funny side-to-side manner.

"I write about the places I wish I'd been to and the adventures I could've had." It was a sad, if not a positive, outlook on life. Pops teased her, and she teased back.

"Go to a nice place now, you silly old bat. If you die, then you die somewhere nice!"

"Or I might never come back!" she retorted, and for a minute Gina could tell that this worried Pops more than he'd ever let on.

Sweet Vigilante

Two hours later she got back to the flat from the hospital. Pops had been given an initial all clear but he had been kept in overnight for observation. He had an impressive list of medical issues that balanced on the tightrope between normal and high. His body was living next door to the danger-zone, and despite the excitement Kenny Loggins tried to inject, this was not a good place to be.

The doctors concluded that Pops had had a mild heart attack, caused by a blood clot in his heart. They didn't seem overly concerned now that he was hooked up to machines that beeped and pinged, but they were also quick to mention that this was still a critical time. The consultant explained how it was a warning, and Pops should take heed and make some drastic changes to his lifestyle. The sweet and fatty treats would have to stop, and he'd need to start a better fitness regime.

Gina thought back to the consultant. He was middle-aged, soft around the middle and thinning on top. His eyes were hard but his smile was warm. He had seemed positive that after tests they would be able to medicate him accordingly so as to stabilise a number of his levels. Despite the vagueness she felt reassured. He had done his job well.

Gina was glad he was in the right place. *That's what everyone usually said, wasn't it?* She thought. But she also longed for him to be back here, shuffling around and getting under her feet.

She grabbed for the packet of her own tablets and chewed a couple down like sweets. She'd been getting on better of late, but this was enough to set her back. She tried to clear her mind, the way she'd learnt to do as a child. If she thought more about Pops then she'd

Jim Ody

be a snivelling mess. Life had toughened her up and beaten a lot of emotions away, but when it came to Pops, she'd be the first to admit she was as soft as shit.

She walked out the door and along to Lynne's flat. She pressed the bell and took a step back.

"Oh Gina," she said, her face dropping. "What is it? Come on in."

Lynne's flat was exactly the same configuration of lounge, kitchen/diner, bathroom, and bedrooms but that was where the resemblance ended. Her tastes were high-end and looked more like a New York townhouse than a flat in an English city.

She had an elegant typewriter that sat in a prominent place on an old mahogany writing desk. It was just for show. She loved the idea that visitors assumed, when they heard she was an author, that she sat tapping away at the typewriter, proudly piling up the pages to her newest manuscript.

"Pops is in hospital," Gina blurted out. She hadn't meant to but the words had been too much.

Lynne was visibly shaken by the words. "Oh, my," she managed and steadied herself into her soft chair.

"He felt faint and collapsed. He had a mini-heart attack… he's fine now… well, still being monitored but I hope to have him back tomorrow, maybe…" her words trailed off. She felt like she was babbling. Lynne was used to jumping into conversations but now she just nodded her head. It was a lot to take in. The two of them really did think they were immortal.

"I…" Lynne began, but realised nothing she had to say seemed important. A silence fell between them. Gina perched herself on the edge of the sofa.

"There has to be some changes," Gina said. "He drinks too much and his diet…"

"I know, but he's a stubborn old fool." She momentarily flashed a little smile. She then glanced over at Gina, and for the first time Gina saw tears in her eyes.

"You have been good for him, G. It is a great relief to me that you are there in that flat with him. He loves you like a grandchild."

Gina nodded. "I know. Don't forget your role too."

Lynne looked away. "My role has always been to push him away," she conceded. "It's not deliberate… or maybe it is. We are great together… I just… you know… I don't want to spoil it."

"Pops knows. I think how you are suits both of you."

From there the conversation lightened up as they retold stories of Pops and the things he'd got up to in his life. It was times like this that you really got to understand a person. To think about the things that stand out in that person's life, and Pops had many. Pops and Lynne had a long chequered past, full of gaps that were never explained. Their friend Abu also appeared often. He was an enigmatic spiritual guy who lived only ten minutes away, and whom Gina visited often. There were times that she saw this strange connection between the three of them but she could never quite put her finger on it, concluding that it was just some fantasy she had invented to provide some radical past for them all.

An hour later and with a promise to keep Lynne updated, Gina headed back to her empty flat.

Jim Ody

No sooner was she in the door, she found herself in the kitchen looking at the bottle of rum that Pops had left on the side. She got up to grab it but then thought better of it.

She didn't contact Abu. Somehow, she was aware he knew already. Lynne was probably speaking to him the minute Gina left her.

She puffed out her cheeks and picked up her paperback. It was some comedy/crime called *Missing Miss Legless*. It didn't seem to be as funny as before, and she struggled to take in the words on the pages. Her mind was all over the place. It was understandable, considering.

She'd missed lunch again and didn't even realise it. Even after she'd brushed her teeth and slipped into bed that night, the hunger pangs were suppressed by worry. The importance of meals had never been drummed into her when she was growing up. They were seen as nothing more than a luxury.

"Good night, Pops," she said out loud to the dark walls of her room. She hoped he was sleeping peacefully in his hospital bed and on the way to a full recovery.

Chapter Three

It was ironic. No sooner had her head touched the pillow and sleep had engulfed her, than the demons in her mind came out to play. They appeared from their hiding places and sneered at her. They laughed and danced, enjoying the pain they brought forth. The projector of her dark upbringing, was eternally injected into her dreams. Even when the dream seemed joyous, she knew even in her lucid state that it would turn out bad.

In one, a puppy nudged her with its wet nose, and she smiled at the innocence of the animal. She reached out to touch its fur, but the man appeared and dragged it away from her. She knew it would be taken to a place, never to return; in another one, a present sat lonely beside her bed. It was wrapped up in paper and a thick ribbon. A tag told her it was hers. She felt so good. Her fingers pulled the ribbon to the side before untying the box, then she ripped away the paper. A white box was left. She opened it up and saw nothing but a pair of eyes sitting on a bed of cotton wool, the crimson liquid soaking around them. In another, she was at the beach, sitting down building a sandcastle. It was huge, and she felt like she'd spent a long time constructing it. Then she saw the panicked faces around her. Fingers pointed, and screams filled the air as she saw the water sucked out farther than she'd ever seen. Hysteria hit and families ran, but it was too late. Out to sea a huge tsunami was heading in to shore and there was nothing any of them could do about it.

It was deep into the night when her eyes shot open. She bolted upright in bed. Sweat had beaded on her forehead and was dripping down her chest and back. She was out of breath and confused.

She'd had a nightmare. A reoccurring scene played out again like a sadistic film director had demanded multiple takes again and again in order to get it right. It was never completely the same. The details changed slightly; faces, expressions, and positions, but essentially the scene was a rough duplication. A poor adaptation of reality.

She remembered the place from before; a long time ago in her past. The smell was so real. She felt the grime underneath her fingernails and the shame that scarred her soul. These were the things that could never change, no matter how hard she tried to lock them away.

Wearing only her vest and pants she walked to the bathroom and splashed water on her face. She looked at her bright red hair in the mirror, spiked in places, long in others. She had a large tattoo of a lipstick kiss above her ear. She'd had it done a while back. She wanted the permanent affection; something she felt had

Sweet Vigilante

been stolen away from her youth. The pain of the tattoo seemed right, and she considered it a beautiful form of self-harm, albeit at the hands of a man who smelt of coffee and cigarettes. There were worse smells in life.

A large portion of her head was shaved but just on the one side and with slightly dishevelled long hair over the rest of it. Sometimes, if her hair was all down, you couldn't see the edgy side of her at all. It was deliberate. Her Jekyll & Hyde, the best analogy of her life. Sometimes she'd smile to herself, and that was just as good.

Her eyes still had the heavy mascara from the day before, and her nose had a large ring through it. She had what was known as *an alternative look,* although so many other people sported it perhaps alternative was now something else. *Who knew?* She thought. All she did know was she liked looking this way, and that was all that mattered. She didn't need a label to know who she was. In fact, she wasn't sure she knew what she was.

Gina liked the contrast of her style. She wanted to look different because inside she felt different. Why try to blend in with others when she knew she was not the same as another living soul?

She went back to bed and tried to get back to sleep, but no matter how hard she tried, sleep was always a little out of reach.

The bright red figures of the clock announced it was 2am. She got up, slipped on some tight black Jeans and leather boots, and grabbed her black biker jacket. She knew the cool air could be unforgiving at this time of the night. But she also knew it to be the thing that made her feel alive.

She slipped out of her front door into the silent corridor. The rest of the building was dead. Her footsteps echoed loudly as she walked down towards the ground floor. She was conscious not to disturb anybody; but she was used to doing this by now. Many nights she woke and wandered out into the wilds.

In the street there was the odd taxi cab taking people home or just cruising for business. Even the hookers looked slightly bored as she nodded to them on Harvey Street. She could tell it was a slow night as none of them had new bruises.

"Stay safe," she said to a girl called Casey. The prostitute shrugged. Staying safe kept her broke, it was taking chances that made her money. That was the nature of the business. But Casey could handle herself. She had to. Street workers are notoriously mistreated. It's as if their chosen vocation allowed punters to abuse them, too, like it was included in the price.

Gina had scars on her knuckles from those types of men. She'd loosened teeth and broken noses for those that didn't understand the simple word *No*. This was nothing new. Men had spent an age throwing their weight around and thinking the mere existence of a penis allowed them to do whatever they pleased. Well, Gina was having none of it – women were taking back their rights, one stupid man at a time. That was a fact.

If you stopped and listened, then the night spoke back to you. There was the deep angry voice of someone; a female scream that could've been in pleasure or pain; a large dog barking in discontent or

Sweet Vigilante

warning, and somewhere a baby was upset. Sirens and car alarms, odd bangs and glass smashing. Some nights heavy rain masked these noises, and often those were the nights where the really bad things happened.

Gina walked among the lost souls that didn't so much own the night, but were victims of it. They would never admit it, but in the small hours if you're still wandering the streets then your life was far from perfect. They considered themselves free. Somehow liberated from life's rules, but they were fooling themselves. Criminals and addicts lie to themselves more than any other people. The reason they often end up in prison was an unconscious desire for routine. Doing bird at Her Majesty's pleasure at least gave them that.

Tonight, she wanted to get lost in the shadows. Perhaps this was her way of coping with the absence of Pops. On some level she wanted to feel that pain again.

"You working?" A confident voice had piped up behind her.

She turned and saw a weasel-faced guy who needed a haircut and a shave. Even then he was about as attractive as a newt. His swagger suggested he was above both. He wanted to get his dirty little hands on her, but hadn't the decency to wash beforehand. She knew his type. A waft of alcohol tried a silent apology that the owner could not admit to. His opportunist eyes were hungry but sad.

"I'm not a whore," she replied evenly and without feeling, though felt a little guilty saying it so defiantly.

"Whatever. Call-girl, escort, hooker? Who gives a fuck, *right*?"

"I do. I'm just out walking."

Jim Ody

"Right. You on your way home? You want company?" He walked closer and brought a wave of day-old sweat with him. Some girls liked the smell of a man's body-odour, and possibly knock-off cologne, but for Gina it brought back too many memories. None of them good. It turned her stomach and made her want to snap the fingers of the owner, one by one.

"No, I don't. Why don't you go back to your wife, huh?" she replied, having already clocked his ring. This married clown, who looked like shit, was out trawling the night searching for a whore. *What sort of life had led him here?* she thought, then dismissed it just as quickly.

He followed her eyes down to his finger. "Oh, this worthless piece of shit? You look like you could give me more than her!" What an awful thing to say. Like marriage was nothing to him at all. A ceremony that must at one point have been the most important thing in his life now reduced to nothing more than an annoyance. Were men really that bad?

Gina stood taller and turned her body. You never wanted to be square on, your balance was compromised. "Really? What, like a broken nose?"

"Don't be like that," he sneered and rubbed his hand on her arm. He then leaned forward with hands looking to own her, however, just as swiftly she head-butted him in the nose, stepped past using his momentum, pulling back to trip him over. He hit the ground hard, holding his face and Gina booted him in the balls.

"Touch me, or another woman like that again, and it will be more than your nose I'll break!"

He made noises of pain. For a second nothing more, either he was too preoccupied by the agony or he thought about trying to be defiant and threaten her, but thought better of it. His small brain finally processed correctly, and he muttered apologies she had no time for. Perhaps next time he'd think better of it. Perhaps next time she'd kill him.

She walked off angry. She fucking hated men ninety percent of the time.

Chapter Four

Gina walked on into the night. The next turn took her down an alleyway between two large and foreboding buildings that pumped out steam from an air-vent. A restaurant-cum-nightclub had closed up for the night and the staff were finally leaving, slowly being swallowed up by the night.

"Yo! Gina!" A chubby guy said, raising his hand to her. He wore a T-shirt with the club emblem on it. He was of medium build but everything about him mumbled *average*.

"Hey, Stu," she replied, holding up a hand, too. She knew he wanted to come over and speak more. She also knew he never would. She intimidated him. He was a sweet guy, but nothing like what she was after. He quickly scuttled away. She knew him from the bookshop where she worked by day. He made a point of coming in when she was around. She suspected he bought books just so he could speak to her. He had a

Sweet Vigilante

mild infatuation, which would disappear the day he touched a real woman's boob.

A hole-in-the-wall food kiosk had more than half a dozen patrons waiting outside in line. A couple more stood chewing down the food, and spit-talked it over each other as they drunkenly chatted and chewed. They were putting the world to rights, unable to stand still and over-engaging with gestures. Not one of them listened to the words of the other. Men could talk, but very few could listen.

As Gina went by, a guy called out, "Gina!" She turned and saw him holding out a takeaway cup.

She turned, walked over to the front of the queue, and accepted it. "On the house," he grinned at her. He was in his fifties. He had a family at home but worked all hours of the day to support them. "Thank you!" she replied. "But you can't give your stuff away, Tony." She placed a banknote in his hand which was worth many times more than the cost of the coffee.

"You're a good person, Gina," he grinned, waving the money away.

"Nah. I just appreciate good people." She disappeared into another alleyway zig-zagging away from where she'd originally come from. The labyrinths of the night.

Gina had a place to go. She ducked down under a low archway and descended some steps into an old building. The lightbulb was on its way out and was flickering with an almost dramatic effect. She could smell the incense before she made it to the door.

She pulled out the key from her pocket, unlocked the door, opened it up and let herself in.

Jim Ody

The haunting sounds of 70s Alice Cooper floated down the hallway. She walked towards the music until she got to the room at the end. The smell of pot was strong. The walls were adorned with scarves and Eastern culture. The music seemed out of place to an outsider, but to Gina it was pure Abu. A spiritual healer. A man who apparently slept less than she did.

There, sitting in an impossible pose was the old Indian man. He was wearing something seemingly fashioned out of a single orange bedsheet, and was in a deep trance. Thick smoke surrounded him. His eyes closed off to the horrors of the world.

"How is he," the guy suddenly said, his eyes still closed. His voice a loud but barely audible whisper over the bass-heavy music.

"He's still alive. He's still critical, but he's a fighter."

Like some sort of reptile, the guy uncoiled himself slowly and gracefully. He opened his eyes, his face deep with lines, and broke into a warm smile.

"His soul shines bright. He still has many years left."

"You think?" Gina replied unsure. She had great faith in Abu, but she had also held Pops in her arms. She had looked deep into his eyes and seen the life seeping out. She never wanted to be in that position again.

She sat down cross-legged and sipped at the black coffee.

Abu stared at her and then at the coffee.

She looked at him deadpan, and winked. She got up made her way to his immaculate kitchen, and poured

Sweet Vigilante

half of her drink into a mug. She walked back in, holding the mug that had *Karma Suits Ya* as a slogan on the side, and handed it to him.

"Your aura is stronger when you share," he said.

"Like yours when you don't bullshit." They both laughed. If Pops was her keeper, and grandfather-figure, then Abu was her spiritual guide. He'd known Pops since dinosaurs roamed the earth, but it was unclear how they had first met.

"You need to look after yourself," he said, taking a sip. "You can't be walking around the city in the dead of night. If nothing else it's not safe for a woman."

"That is a highly sexist thing to say," she pointed out. "I expect better of you!"

He grinned. "I know. Statistically, a guy in his twenties is of a higher risk bracket, but you know what I mean. It doesn't make the world any safer for you."

"I can look after myself."

"I know you can. But what if they have a weapon?"

"Then it's more of a challenge. And they'll more than likely need hospital treatment."

Abu stretched out his arms. "I know you're listening. And I know you're stubborn!"

"Just like Pops," she smiled, her mind switching to him.

"Just like Pops," Abu agreed, nodding his head and sipping the coffee.

Dropping the subject, they talked more generally before their cups were empty, good-byes were said, and Gina was back off into the night and heading home.

She wondered whether life would give her more of a purpose or whether she'd remain in this cycle until she was the same age as Pops, but with no one to look after her. She hated to look into the future.

Chapter Five

16 Years ago…

She turned around and watched her mother's car leave the huge driveway of the boarding school. In her hand she held dear her rabbit. Her other arm made an awkward attempt at a wave, but she knew her mother wouldn't be watching.

She heard voices and turned to see a group of girls snickering at her and making cry-baby faces.

"Boo-hoo!" a few of them mocked, pretending to cry complete with circular hand movements near their eyes.

"Admit it, Screamer-Gina, you're not wanted by your mother, and you're not wanted here!" The tallest of the group said, her face hard and bitter.

"Yeah! Go home!" another girl said, stepping out from behind the girl. She was smaller, but known for her big mouth.

Gina hated them so much, and she'd been really anxious to come back this term. It seemed that no matter where she was, she always got in the way, or was nothing but a frustration to those around her. These girls definitely hated her. She felt the lump in her throat. From nowhere it appeared and only made her feel even worse. There was no hiding her feelings. She looked past the girls and saw her friend hiding in the shadows, too scared to show herself.

"Why did you even come back?" another girl said. Like Gina had a choice, Gina wanted to shout at them. She wanted to stand up on something and scream at the top of her lungs that this was the last place she wanted to be. But then what? Everyone would laugh and the Head Mistress would stride out and scold her, and send her off to Mr Munroe for discipline. Nobody wanted to go to him. She'd heard stories about him, and none of them were good.

Gina looked up at the old building. The gothic structure was huge. It was dark and creepy with spiky architecture wherever you looked. Strange gargoyles sat high up under the roof's edges watching them, almost waiting to come to life and carry off a child that strayed onto one of the many paths alone.

"Look at her!" the original leader said. "Pathetic."

Gina looked hard at the roof and ignored the comment and the constant evil stares. She felt such anger inside. It was life. It started in the bottom of her new leather shoes, slowly worked its way up her legs, her body, and eventually into her brain. She wanted it so badly. Then she saw it. A movement. Only slight and so far away that it could easily have been her eyes playing tricks on her.

A slate moved. And then it fell.

"What are you even –" Suddenly she screamed as the tile missed her by a foot. The other girls reacted too, jumping back in a squeal, then turning to go into the building. Rats leaving their leader as she too, turned and ran off.

She knew that this meant nothing. It was but a pause in their games and later on they'd start again. She looked up, and then looked back down at the tile and had to wonder: *Did I do that?*

She really couldn't be sure.

Then, out of the darkness her friend appeared.

"Hi, Gina. Are you okay?" Her weak smile showed she knew the answer, but she also wanted to show her support.

"I guess so. You?"

She nodded. "That was close… Come on, let's get you settled back in." She grabbed one of the bags, and the two girls walked into the huge building. What had happened was at the forefront of their minds, but neither of them wanted to bring it up.

Chapter Six

Gina didn't need to set an alarm; her nightmares woke her up with regularity better than any piercing sound of an alarm clock.

She knew of people who loved the excitement of twisted dreams. In the morning they would wake and be thrilled as they thought about the horrors they'd endured, acting like they'd watched a movie instead of the near reality of a dream. For Gina life wasn't like this, as her dreams closely resembled her past. Her day started only with regrets over what had happened to Tommy.

She never got used to the silent movie that played back, flashing like a cinefilm. Pops had suggested on more than one occasion that she needed to visit somebody. Sit down and talk through her past but she really didn't want to do that. It was bad enough that she had to revisit the past in her dreams, so to deliberately dig them up in her waking day filled her with too much anxiety. Lynne suggested she write her experiences down, either in the form of a personal memoir, or even scene by scene, and how it made her feel, but again it would force her back there. Then Abu had suggested meditation. He taught her ways to bury the hatred into a box in her mind, then lock the door to the room it was in and to walk away. That was something she could do, and despite Pops and Lynne disagreeing with this decision she did it anyway. It was the easy option, the one with the least pain.

If she was honest, the lid to the box wasn't closed up fully, and the door to the room was open as the dark thoughts were still able to creep and crawl out.

Gina checked her phone for missed calls from the hospital, and when she saw there weren't any, she closed her eyes in relief. She momentarily thought about ringing them but knew it would take an age to find someone who had any information. If there was an issue then they would call. She just wanted that extra peace of mind.

She didn't want a lonely breakfast in the flat; it felt too big and quiet without Pops. He was an early bird up at the crack of dawn. He would be found cooking his favourite meal of the day which invariably was something fried, and unhealthy, and then swilled down with strong black coffee. That would have to change. He'd have to start looking after himself. This was a wake-up call.

The next place she'd normally go was an American-style diner called Max it Up, which was owned by another friend of Pops' called Max. She hated to admit it, but she didn't want to have to go through the story of Pops again with him. He was a great guy, but she wanted to collect her thoughts and not have sympathetic looks thrown her way.

Instead, Gina left early and grabbed a coffee and muffin from the artisan coffee shop downtown. She didn't spend her money on much, but for coffee she was happy to be frivolous with her cash. She had some fleeting justification that some third-world farmer was benefiting from her decision.

The coffee shop was high end. Dark woods and metallic furnishings. She sat on the sofa and pulled out her book for another go at being amused. For a while it worked, until she remembered Pops. The way he looked hooked up to the machines. It was not something that she'd ever get used to. He looked so vulnerable and weak; his skin deathly grey.

She gazed out of the window at nothing in particular. The world moved on quickly with people all in a rush to be someplace. There was a sadness that they carried on blissfully unaware of the wonderful man who was laid out in a hospital bed. Life moved on. That was what it did.

And then she saw him scurry across the road towards her. Not Pops but the guy from the dark shadows. The one she'd left on his back clutching his balls in pain.

It was easy to notice his rat features even with the larger bruised nose. She almost ducked but remembered she was wearing her glasses and had her trilby hat on covering her red hair, now pulled back. She was artist Gina blending into the wash of people.

She sometimes thought of her alter-ego as a separate person and wondered what her life would be

Sweet Vigilante

like: night-prowling Gina was probably comatose someplace. Half-wrapped up in a bedsheet, a hot guy was snoring next to her and an empty Jim Beam bottle had fallen on the floor. She'd be drenched in dry blood, sex, and alcohol. Whereas, daytime Gina Chandler was smartly dressed and ready for her job in the second-hand book shop. She was a mixture of styles; perhaps sophisticated Emo might be some hip tag. Maybe she was considered some hipster sub-genre. Maybe. She really couldn't care less.

Rat-face glanced over but appeared more embarrassed, not as a result of recognition but by being spied by a pretty lady. And Gina was nothing short of being a pretty lady. Rat-face wasn't much to look at before last night. His bruised nose was now swollen and rounded his usual sharp features, although the bruising did not. She looked away ready to forget him, but instead decided against it. She'd probably see him again. In her experience, slimeballs had short memories.

She grabbed her phone and sent off a text. The person was incredibly important to her. Someone who stopped her from being pulled into the police station for her violent acts. His name was Rogers. He worked in a special agency affiliated with the police. He was the person who Gina contacted when she needed a quick response. He knew all about her and how she helped the city. He paved the way for her to do what she did. Only a few people knew, and they had made the commercial decision that it was for the greater good of the city. The bigger picture – although it was also said that her position would be constantly reviewed.

Jim Ody

Within a few minutes he responded to tell her there was nothing for her to be worried about. She knew she always ran the risk of being pulled in by officers unaware of what she did, and Rogers admitted it might be hard to get her released, although it was unlikely she'd ever be charged. He always ended his message the same way.
Try not to kill anyone, Gina.
It always made her smile. It was something she could never confirm. So she responded the same way she always did:
I'll try. x
The young guy behind the counter looked like he'd been trying to pluck up the courage to speak to her. He was close to burning up red every time she glanced at him, and his tongue was ready to trip over any words he dared to utter if he only had the balls to speak. He wasn't bad looking, but she didn't have time for romance. To her it was a wasted feeling that only left you at risk by dropping your guard. She wasn't going to make that mistake again. Pops and her work colleagues gave her the male friendship she desired, and when she wanted to have sex, she went out and chose a man. It sounded animalistic, but she wanted no-strings-attached sex, which was incredibly easy to find. Always void of tenderness; often rough and quick. It was enough to scratch her itch. Most disappeared just as quickly as the act itself. That wasn't always a bad thing.

She said goodbye and walked out and down the road. It was a five-minute walk to the side street and the bookshop.

Sweet Vigilante

Baxter's Books was a fairly large book shop even if it was tucked away like a dirty little secret. It was almost as big as a Waterstones but made to look rustic. Baxter, the owner, had bought the bookshop from a drunkard who had let the place go downhill. The guy wanted out and practically gave the shop, including its stock, away for a steal. Baxter gutted the place and fixed it up to something that was quirky and hip. Sure, it had hipster written all over it and half of their clientele could be described as such, but so what? That was the area where they lived. Young professional. These weren't the e-Readers, wearing Fitbit watches and sipping Evian 24/7. These were lovers of the paperback who wanted them previously read, their pages discoloured, and the smell permeating to their nostrils like the residual souls from previous readers, sucked and held into the book forever. They wore their tortoiseshell glasses and had antique watches and sipped coffee made from beans that had been through the digestive system of Indonesian palm civet cats because the taste was far superior to that of Starbucks – or so they professed. They searched for the rarities, and within the bookshop café they could elaborate on the plots from the classics and the true meanings behind them, not the false opinions of stuffy professors stuck in the past. They'd find new authors that were ground-breaking and considered *a contemporary voice of a new generation*; and they'd instigate a cult-like following to something quirky that was scandalously shunned by literary critics. Some men with floppy hair, woollen hats, and skinny jeans would hang around the various book groups that would meet up in a hope that they would get to have a one-on-one discussion with one of the members – specifically within the comforts of a bed and unclothed. They'd carry around a beat up copy of their favourite book with many passages underlined. They glance over these whilst sipping their oat-milk lattes, memorising them word-for-word so they could repeat them at a later date at a dinner party for the sole purpose of looking interesting. They were heavily opinionated in regards to the classics, sometimes dismissive although appreciative of the path that had been laid for books they considered far superior.

So many characters within the city.

Gina loved her job. Whether she was sorting out books that had been brought in, stock checking, changing the window display, serving behind the counter, or updating/marketing the shop on social media, it was all fun to her.

"You're looking good, Gina!" Baxter winked at her as he walked by with a wobbling tower of books. He was flirtatious but just in a friendly way. To others this might sound like a come-on, but not to Gina – that was just Baxter. He had a fiancée who he loved dearly, and he would comment the same to Gina whether they were alone or he was standing next to his fiancée and holding her hand.

"Thanks," she smiled. It was always nice to hear. He was a good-looking guy after all. Sometimes she wished there was more to his words but knew nothing good would ever come of it.

She placed the Jack Ketchum book back on the shelf and smiled. Some people found the author too dark and graphic, but to her that was just what the

Sweet Vigilante

world was like. Why sugar coat everything? The likes of Caroline Kepnes and CJ Skuse had successfully gate-crashed literary commercialism with their coarse, brash, and genuinely honest narratives. Not so much a breath of fresh air, as breath reeking of stale-coffee and the mutual oral escapades from the night before.

She turned around and was about to take a break when she saw a guy shaking his head and looking lost. Inside she laughed. This guy was out of place in a bookshop. He looked like he would've preferred to be at a cricket match, or spouting out sexual remarks with his buddies over a cold one. He was middle-aged – maybe older – and had floppy hair and a thick unkempt beard. He had jowls that wobbled and a bulbous nose probably from drink. He was a big and imposing guy.

"Hi! Can I help you?" she asked, walking towards him. This was another part of the job that she enjoyed. In a bookshop people liked to browse, unsure of what they wanted. They were always open to recommendations. Small things attracted different people.

He flapped his arms against his legs in frustration. It was clear he wasn't buying a book for himself.

"Damned if I know. She wants a book. She tells me to surprise her... I just don't get it. Every year I get her wine and flowers. She likes that. But this year, no, she's all about surprises... I got a surprise for her, maybe I get her some book on divorce! Ha-ha! *How's that for your surprise!* I'll laugh!"

Gina did that false chuckle saved for those awkward types of situations. It had been perfected so as people unknown to her would be none the wiser.

"What books does she read?"

Jim Ody

He made a huge gesture shrugging and throwing his large hands up. "Damned if I know," he said again. "She's in bed not long after she's eaten, who knows what she's looking at in bed! Probably some erotic shit… pardon my French." He added the last bit as an afterthought. He was full on with what he considered to be charm. Perhaps at some stage in his life he'd had success, though she doubted that had been for quite some time. She also suspected the only French he knew was *ménage á trois*.

There was something about him. Gina couldn't put her finger on it but it was like she knew him. A spark deep within her brain had started.

"Does she read fiction?" she said but her mind was running in and out of memory rooms. Her customer service autopilot took over.

"Probably, she's good at making shit up! Ha-ha!" he laughed out loud at that. Probably too loud, as if he needed to tell everyone it was a joke.

She pointed over to the chart section. They stocked a number of brand new books as well as old. This worked really well pulling in two separate types of customers – the ones who want cheap second-hand books, and the ones hungry for popular new books. They even had a lending section that could be joined for a few pounds a year. Baxter was all about new ideas.

This guy had a slight limp and a large barrel belly on him. He made a grab for a book, but really it could've been a tin of kidney beans such was his lack of interest. He flipped the pages in that speedy way that told you he'd taken in nothing. His disinterest was more evident when he dropped it. With a huge huff he bent and scooped it up.

The back of his shirt rode up, flashing a roll of fat around his midsection. But on the roll was a tattoo. The bottom of a large eagle. The long sharp talons of the bird of prey.

Gina gasped audibly, shocked at the sight. Her breathing became rapid and it was hard for her to take in air. She tried but her lungs felt solid.

In a matter of moments flashes appeared, changing the images to a skinnier version of this man; naked, without the beard, and sneering up at her. The same tattoo sat across his lower back. She'd been made to touch it. An awful sensory memory appeared from nowhere: the taste of him sour in her mouth.

"You okay?" Zee, the junior of the shop asked, running to her. His voice at first was distant like it was in another building, then it had a strange echo to it.

Gina realised that she was sitting on the floor and was rubbing her head. She was dizzy, and struggling to focus. She lost a few moments.

The guy had now gone. The book remained on the floor near her. His wife would get the wine and flowers again this year.

"Baxter!" Zee called. "Gina's had a fall."

"Where'd he go?" Gina said, disorientated.

"Who? Baxter?"

"No, the guy. The large guy? I was talking to him."

"He's gone," Zee said. "He made an exit. I guess he didn't like your customer service!"

Gina shot him a look but noticed that Zee was joking.

Jim Ody

"You okay?" Baxter said concerned. "What happened?"

"I'm fine. It's probably just stress." Gina pulled out her phone. "Look, Baxter, can I take an early lunch? Pops is in hospital. I want to see him."

"What!! Why didn't you tell me earlier? Yes, go!"

"I'll be back later… I just…"

"Don't be stupid. We can cope. Take the rest of the day off. Wish him well from us, will ya?"

They all knew Pops. He often came in and was well liked by everyone in the shop. Baxter looked like he had been told his own father was in hospital, such were his feelings for the old man.

Some days Pops would turn up. He'd grab a cappuccino, assuming it to be slightly continental, then he'd take out an Agatha Christie novel and read. However he often struggled to finish a chapter as Baxter or other members of staff would pull up a chair and speak to him. Pops joked that he barely got any reading done there, but deep down he loved the fuss. And of course, the real reason he was there was to check up on Gina.

Now she would check up on him.

Gina got up. She had no missed calls.

She hadn't slept much last night, so the stress and lack of sleep could easily have made her see things.

Things that she never wanted to see again. He could've been an innocent guy with a similar tattoo. Or maybe he didn't even have one. Sleep deprivation could easily have created it.

"Thanks guys!" she called as she walked out. They smiled, but she saw the worry behind them.

Sweet Vigilante

She jumped onto a bus and headed straight to the hospital. In the city, public transport was so much more efficient. The buses ran every ten minutes, and with their own lanes got you around the city much quicker than a car. Her car was there in case she needed it. *Really* needed it someday.

She wasn't a fan of buses, though, so took taxi cabs most places a little too far to walk.

She thanked the cab driver who nodded. It was unusual to find one who remained quiet. Most of them liked the sound of their own voices and thought nothing of talking non-stop, whether or not you cared to listen. If she was on a tv game show, then she would have a cab driver on her team. They knew everything. Apart from getting a better paid job.

Hospitals were always busy. There was a high chance that we'd all visit one a dozen or so times in our lifetime. Not many other places could boast that. Often babies were born there, and unfortunately people died there, too. In between were visits to A&E, or for any number of operations, whether routine or not, throughout a person's lifespan. Very rarely were they a place of excitement or enjoyment, but still they remained just as important today as they did hundreds of years ago. Technology cannot change everything.

The strong smell of anti-bacterial cleaner was everywhere. At first it was overpowering. Its job was to be the tough defence against the germs and bacteria, not to mention infections, diseases, and death, that silently ghosts the hallways. Suddenly it's not so bad.

Gina's first stop had been to visit the hospital shop and she'd bought chocolate and a paper for him. She figured he needed a treat before he started his health kick. With the gifts in hand, she walked up the wide staircase, along the corridor, and towards his ward.

She pushed open the door to his room, and the old man grinned at her. He looked a lot better than the last time she'd seen him.

"There she is!" he laughed. "Lovely Gina!"

"Hey Pops! How you doin'?"

He nodded. "I been better, kid, but then I'm old! This is a taste of what's to come, I guess!"

"They looking after you?"

"I've got a couple of young nurses that check on me regularly, so I really can't complain!"

She sat on the edge of the bed and held his hand. It felt cold, leathery, and like she was grabbing on to bones.

"You know we're making changes, right?" she said to him. "Food and drink." She tried to look serious, but she struggled with the overwhelming relief of his looking like he could jump out of bed there and then and do some sort of jig around the room.

"Here we go!" But there was jest in his response, especially as his gaze dropped to the chocolate bar she'd bought him.

"That will be your last!" she waggled an authoritative finger at him. "They will only be on special occasions after that."

"At my age I might not have many special occasions left!"

She rolled her eyes before adding, "You have to look after yourself, and don't come that with me, I know you seem to think you're immortal!"

Sweet Vigilante

He laughed hard at that. It ended in a couple of deep chesty coughs, and he struggled to get his breath.

"I guess not..." he managed, and then swallowed and continued. "Gina look, open that drawer there," his wrinkled hand was still huge but there seemed less meat on it than there had been a few days ago. She hated the mortal inevitability of it all.

She reached over and grabbed it.

"What am I looking at?"

"Open the box there."

She opened it up and saw the thick ring that seemed too large and showy for his pale digits.

"Your class ring," she said out loud. He'd been raised in America, but had come over to England years ago and settled here.

He nodded. "Open the other side."

She did as she was told, and there, almost forgotten, was a smaller more feminine version.

"I want you to look after these for me," he said with a serious face.

"You'll be out soon, maybe even today!" she said, feeling her throat choke up, and then her eyes began to fill. She knew this was out of hope rather than anything else. Despite how well he looked, she knew things had been serious.

He just shrugged. "Maybe I will, and maybe I won't. But still look after these, yeah?"

She nodded and flung her arms around him. Her tears dripped onto him. He seemed like he'd break if she hugged him too hard.

"Don't be silly, old man. Stay strong. You'll be home soon."

"Maybe," he said again, and she wondered whether he knew more than he was letting on.

They chatted for a little while before a nurse came in, interrupting the moment and explained that Pops had to have more tests done.

"I'll be back later," Gina said, kissing him on the cheek.

"I look forward to it," he replied as she walked out.

To her something just didn't feel right.

When she got back from the hospital, she once again noticed the flat was a lonely place for her. She sat back in the battered leather chair where Pops would normally rest and ate down some Pot Noodles. They were her comfort food. She ate apples and salads normally, washing it down with bottled water in some unconscious notion that it purified the horrors that she'd endured growing up. She certainly allowed herself treats but made sure she ate naturally and exercised daily to keep herself in tiptop condition. Some days it was like she was in training for an event she wasn't aware of.

Her bare feet were curled up under her as she twisted the new ring on her finger, and glanced at the photo of the two of them that hung on the wall adjacent to the television.

The face of the man today was there in her mind. Exhausted, she closed her eyes and held the ring tightly. It wasn't long before she drifted off into a deep sleep.

She was transported back there again. She was young and vulnerable. A million miles away from the woman she was today.

Sweet Vigilante

Chapter Seven

He stood there across the street from her flat the same way he did every so often. He took another long drag from his cigarette and put his head back to blow the plume of smoke into the air above. He didn't realise it, but it was an alpha-male trait. In the animal kingdom it could be likened to a lion putting back its head before roaring, signaling to the rest of those around that he was in charge. He idly flicked the butt of the cigarette and took a quick swig of his coffee that he held in a takeout cup.

He pretended to send a text message, but he was actually taking a photograph of her. He'd upload it to his hard drive later on. He liked to see any changes she made to her appearance. She liked to be different. He scoffed at the thought. She thought she was better than everyone else.

Today she had her hair pulled back and wore a hat. It annoyed him because for most people it would look ridiculous, but on her it looked fine. How, he had no

Sweet Vigilante

clue. A hat on top of bright red hair and arms that bore sleeves of tattoos shouldn't work. But it bloody did.

He began to walk in parallel with her but on the other side of the street. He watched her glance around and go back to keeping her head down in front of her. She never saw him. He always knew when she was about to look over, and he'd dart in front of someone to obscure her view. He'd grin to himself at how clever he was, but more so because he knew she didn't know. This gave him the upper hand. No matter how good she thought she was, he knew he remained one step ahead.

She trotted across the road as cars and vans were at a standstill. The commuter traffic in the city was getting worse.

He watched as she walked between people and eventually disappeared into an independent coffee shop. It was an interesting choice seeing as they sold coffee where she worked. It was these little things that kept him guessing. She kept him on his toes. HE liked that.

But more than anything else in the world, he loved the fact that he knew all about her and she didn't realise.

He knew she slipped out at night and thought she was fucking Wonder Woman. She took on stupid men who thought they knew best and eventually kicked their arses. He had seen it a few times, but of course she never saw him.

That would eventually be her downfall. He was a shadow and she was the light. You can't kill a shadow. You can only kill the light.

He drained his coffee and threw it in a looping arc

Jim Ody

into the nearest bin. A woman looked at him and grinned. He winked at her, and she blushed. He merged back into the sea of people unnoticed.

Chapter Eight

15 years ago

Darkness surrounded her. Nothing was familiar and her future seemed in doubt. She couldn't understand what was happening. When was her mother coming back?

Slowly she backed up against the damp wall next to the bed and hugged her knees tightly. There was little comfort in doing this, but what else did she have? Her beloved toy bunny had been ripped apart in front of her. He was the last attachment to her old life – ruined. She sort of knew he wasn't real, but he'd been a friend nevertheless; someone to talk to and share her life with. To see the look of glee in their faces, as the arms and legs came away from his body. It was awful. She felt like it was happening to a real person. She broke down at the act. They didn't even let her hold his pieces; they just taunted her with them, laughing and joking before they took them outside, and set his remains alight. She silently cried for him, and for her own loss. She was now truly alone.

For months she woke up screaming for him, but he was never there. The mere thought of what they had done was enough to buckle her legs from under her and render her paralysed.

She was in one of the attic rooms. The ones with the thick walls that muffled the screams from within.

The sound of the footsteps coming up the stairs scared her. Each held the weight of evil. She knew what it represented. She gulped back tears. She had to be strong. It was the only way to get through it. Could she get through it? She knew if she was ever to get away then she'd have to.

The door burst open, knocking over the chair she'd used in a feeble attempt at a barricade. She knew it wouldn't stop him, but at least if she was sleeping, she'd know he was there. More than once she'd woken to see those eyes looking at her in a way a man should never look at a child. She could never relax. The callused touch of his rough hands, followed by the suffocating weight of his body on top of her. She didn't understand what was happening, it was all too confusing.

"What is this?" the voice boomed out full of anger. "And not eating your dinner, too! You think you can just do as you please?" It was rhetorical. She'd seen what happened to children who answered back.

It wasn't just tooth-fairies that took away teeth.

With the logic of an ostrich, she buried her head deeply between her knees, hiding as much as possible. Feeble and cowardly. She cowered as she heard him

Sweet Vigilante

come close. She smelt his fetid breath; a mix of stale coffee and cigarettes. It mixed in with the onion-sweat that rose defiantly from the dirty crevices of his body.

"Lewis told me what you did," he said slowly and calculatingly. You could almost detect the sound of pleasure as he knew he would have to deal out a punishment. Somehow shifting the blame to her. He tried to make out he wasn't enjoying this but he had no choice.

"No... No..." she sobbed. She knew she'd not done anything wrong other than leave some food. Lewis had disliked her immensely since the day she'd arrived. His jealousy was evident albeit unwarranted; it was obvious he was already the favourite, receiving far more privileges than any of the children. He was slightly older and never received a beating.

They called the man Jeff, but he made her call him Pa. He pulled at Gina roughly, and she scrambled to her feet, barely able to keep her balance. Submissively, and like a condemned prisoner, she followed him down the stairs and outside to the shed. Now brainwashed through punishment, he knew she'd obediently follow. The power was there after he broke them. They tried to run only once.

The quietness of the countryside was now eerie and a reminder of just how far away she was from civilisation. There was a cold bite to her bare arms, and she longed for invisible arms to reach out from the trees and take her away.

She was shoved through the door so hard she lost her balance. She crumpled to the ground and grazed her arm. She reached out for the mattress. She knew it was dirty, soiled with blood and bodily fluids, but despite that, there was a comfort versus the dirt of the floor. She'd been here so often that it almost felt like home. A familiar resignation washed over her. She would be here for the night, maybe longer.

He followed her in and made her undress. Her mind left her body as she became limp and he possessed her.

Later when he turned his back to pull up his trousers, she saw that tattoo again. She hated the sight of it. It represented only abuse. A signature of non-consensual dominance.

This was no longer a place to be sent for rule-breaking, but rather a place for him to do whatever he so desired. Made-up accusations to warrant his actions. Always making out it wasn't his fault. Gina began to forget the various reasons for each isolation. The first few times the trivial excuses upset her. How could people banish her from the normal comforts of life for answering back, refusing to say prayers, or for making a mess? But slowly she came to realise that it wasn't always about the small instances but rather as a deterrent for escalating to worse crimes. It was, after all, a show of power by Jeff, and his wives Lyndsey and Vicky, too. The additional wife was strange at first, but like most things became completely natural until it was the norm to her.

She remembered that first time. When he had finally left, how she sat there shivering and crying. She felt disgusted and ashamed for something she hadn't done. She was confused. The rules were vague, and she was mad at herself for not learning them properly. She wanted a parent to cuddle her, but she knew she'd been abandoned by her mother. She didn't know how long she would be there, nor could she be sure she would ever be let out. Her bunny was nothing but ash in the wind – maybe he had been the lucky one to escape all of this. She had nothing but the voices in her head to keep her company. Most of the time they weren't enough. Her nails found a home in digging into her forearms and drawing blood. At first she didn't know she was doing it, and then eventually the pain gave her a strange sort of comfort.

For the first four hours all she had was a bottle of water. Then she was given a couple of biscuits. Not huge American cookies, but the small plain digestives that come in a packet. At one time she would've turned her nose up at them, instead wanting the ones with chocolate on them, but now she was thankful and savoured the taste.

It was the next morning before she was let out. Her bones felt the damp deep inside, and she had a permanent chill running through her.

Dragged away from the isolation shed, she was flung back into the room with the other children. Each one of them a sorry sight. Eyes filled with more sorrow than should ever be evident in children. Each knew what she'd been through. There was an equal empathic sadness towards her, but an underlying relief that it had not been them this time.

Next time, it may well be. They sobbed together.

Happiness couldn't find their house. The devil kept it away. This was its playground and there was nothing anyone could do about it.

Chapter Nine

Gina woke up with a start and found she'd fallen asleep in the chair. She could see the house from her past like it was in front of her. It had been years, and the vision of that evil place had been locked away deep in her memory. But the tattoo was still there, fresh in her mind. An aching reminder.

It was late afternoon but she suddenly had a feeling she'd not had before. An obsession to go and find that place. The one from her nightmares.

For many nights as a child, she'd fantasised about leaving that place. When she finally did, she never looked back. The mere thought of it scared her. She'd continued to look over her shoulder for years. Right up until recently.

But now, in a complete plot change, she wanted to go back. She was bigger and stronger now. She had to get revenge. But that was it. She hated to admit it even to herself, but she was not the only victim. The guilt

Sweet Vigilante

was worse than remembering the pain. She'd escaped, but others hadn't been so strong.

She was haunted by the visions of Tommy. Sweet little Tommy. He was a few years younger. He cried at night and often wet himself. He spent many nights in the shed. The next day he would refuse to leave her side. She was his big sister. He had a way of looking up to her. Snot dripping from a nostril enlarged from a beating, he'd try to smile as he snuggled into her.

"Don't cry, Tommy," she'd say. "They'll come and get you again if you're not strong."

At first, and like all of them, he'd been filled with hope. He was confused, but told her his mum was ill. He wasn't sure what was wrong with her but was convinced that when she was better, she was coming to get him. From there his eyes looked off faraway, the truth, the hopeful possibility, and the fantasy all merged together. She saw that look, the one that was no longer based on reality and she let him believe. He smiled when he said his mum was going to buy him a new bike, a dog, and sweets, and he'd go to the beach, and stay in their new house by the sea. She nodded happily to him but knew his mum was never coming back. Deep down she was sure Tommy knew she was never coming back either.

She'd never had any friends. She'd been shipped off on a bus to a school but had never integrated well with the other kids, and she was excluded from parties and socials. She would've loved to have had a little brother, so Tommy filled that gap for her. She wanted to take him with her, but that night when she'd made her escape, there was no way to get him.

Jim Ody

That was the hardest thing about it all. She felt like she'd abandoned him just like his mum had. But if she'd gone into the house to get him, there would be no way she could leave the others. The poor innocent souls couldn't be chosen. And the more of them she chose to save, the more noise and likelihood of them all being caught.

Then she never would've escaped. She probably would've died there.

But she had a feeling that Tommy didn't last much longer. He wasn't strong. He was the runt of the litter, born to be a victim. It stood to reason. He would be buried somewhere in the garden. Nothing to mark a sweet little body that lay forgotten and lifeless below the ground.

Tommy wouldn't have got to see his mum again. He never got to see the house by the sea, go to the beach, see his bike, new dog, or eat the sweets. Her decision to leave had signed an invisible death warrant, and every few days it was this that kept her up at night.

Poor Tommy. Poor sweet little Tommy.

But this was now. She couldn't explain what she was about to do, the rationale of jumping into her car and driving off on a whim to find that hell house. Did she really think she could find it after all these years? Even if she was able to somehow unlock the memories, the roads and surrounding area would've changed. But she had this sudden optimism that she couldn't explain. She was on a mission. She was compelled to follow her senses and just drive.

She grabbed a bottle of water and left the flat, but not before blowing a kiss to the picture of Pops. She checked her phone again, just in case the hospital had called. They hadn't.

Her car was an old Honda, considered a good model when it was released, but now twenty years since it rolled off the production line at Swindon, it showed signs of a tough life. Everything about it showed its age. Even the steering wheel had wear in the places that her ringed fingers rubbed. The windows took an age to go down and the wipers were okay as long as there was no rain and they remained still. It had been a solid red colour when new, but now it was faded to an unnatural pale pink. It was as if the car was dying of old age, too, right before her eyes.

She was focused on the road ahead trying to channel something unknown from within whilst obeying the laws of the highway. Perhaps she was being stupid, a mixture of something vaguely psychosomatic and something nostalgic all mixed up with some spirituality she unconsciously picked up from Abu.

She surmised that whilst she didn't know the exact location, a person who spent enough time in an area would know deep inside the rough direction of it. An inner compass. No sooner had the idea entered her mind, she had already laughed it off. *Who was she kidding?*

To begin with, she turned into a couple of streets, and then lanes leading out of the city, but it felt wrong. Perhaps a sixth sense that she'd tapped into. Or maybe her mind was still trying to repress her thoughts. She felt stupid. What the hell was she doing? Shouldn't she just go back to the flat and sit by the phone to wait for the hospital to call?

Jim Ody

She relaxed a little, tried to clear her mind and made sure she didn't force or influence her thoughts. She couldn't explain it, but a whisper in her head told her which turn to take until finally she was going out of the city and heading deep into the countryside. It was like connecting with energy that she'd never tried to use before. She'd heard of neuroscientists who spoke of the untapped potential of the human brain, and even within the dedicated field there was a lot of conflict on the subject. You could read into it any which way you choose. Some say there is so much more we can achieve if we trained ourselves, and others dismiss these claims by suggesting that some people are just born with extreme capabilities, and it's unrealistic to think that everyone can do the same, citing that not everyone can be Einstein. Gina wondered whether some people were just born with special powers.

The road ahead was long and straight, dipping every now and then, and covered by trees that appeared to lean over and touch branches like outstretched arms. On a normal level, everything was new. She'd had no reason to leave the city, other than on the odd trip to the coast, but that was in the opposite direction. Perhaps part of her had deliberately kept this behind her.

Gina felt alive driving without a known purpose. It was liberating and so out of character. For someone so used to structure and routine, this felt almost foolhardy.

A huge wind turbine was on her left in a field, another in a field next to it. The huge propellers moved round slowly. There was something familiar about it.

Sweet Vigilante

The domineering structure that looked like something out of the book *War of The Worlds*, laying dormant until such a time it kicked into action to help destroy those on earth. She had a flashback to seeing it years before, and thinking then how scary they looked. –That was before she'd ever been aware of the book (or the following film adaptations).

At the weekends, some people often chose to drive out into the country and be one with nature, but for her it held no attraction. She was a city rat now enjoying living in the pockets of others. She had no desire to live out in a place where your screams could not be heard. She'd already been there, done that, and got the scars. This ideology of a peaceful sanctuary was lost on her.

Instinctively, her weight pushed down with her right foot on the brake. Life slowed down, then reality, and memory collided in slow-motion. She felt herself gasp.

A beat-up people-carrier pulled out from a dirt drive up ahead. A battered post box sat in front of a couple of large trees. Gina rolled the car into a make-shift layby on the other side of the road and got out. With shaky hands on her hips, she glanced down the driveway towards a house.

She looked all around and even glanced into the sky above. It looked so large. She was used to tall buildings and blocks of flats busying her view of above. The perspective was always hard to work out. You just felt small and inconsequential. Here, she just felt more exposed and lost.

The house was unsightly against the beauty of the landscape, perhaps not to others but to her it made her feel sick in the stomach.

Jim Ody

She felt eyes on her. She imagined whispers between small lips into the ears of elders. Their sneering faces bearing teeth and looking down the barrel of a shotgun at her. Large arms grabbing her and dragging her whilst she kicked and screamed.

Gina turned around in a full three-sixty. She was alone. However, she knew in the countryside even when it appeared so, you were never alone. Predators lay in wait all around you. In the city it was the same, except these were in human form and thought they ruled the roost in the night.

Somewhere deep within the hidden vault of her mind everything appeared familiar. The formation of bushes, trees, and even the post box, but for the most part everything was still hazy with fuzzy edges. Her memories were an old faded picture that had been folded so much that white lines had appeared like they were part of the photograph.

Only six years ago this had been her home. Although the word home had never seemed right. Prison was far more apt.

Taking in a deep breath she walked down the drive. As she got closer to the house her heart rate quickened, and she felt sick to her stomach. She held comfort in the knowledge of the large knife in the sheath on her belt. She'd used it before, and she'd use it again.

Her pace quickened as she got a few feet away. Adrenaline now seeped into her veins and her heart pumped it all around her body. Her head snapped back and forth as she wondered whether she was being watched. Part of her didn't care. She was bigger now. Wiser and stronger. She'd learnt mixed martial arts

Sweet Vigilante

down at her gym. A small, grimy establishment full of tough men with hearts of gold. She'd been only too keen to learn from them all until she was able to take them on, and beat them at their own disciplines. Height and strength were an advantage, but speed and technique were even better. When she had learnt enough techniques, she returned only for fitness and to keep sharp. She had never been motivated enough to fight other women she knew nothing about.

She rapped a couple of times on the old wooden doorframe. White chips of paint fluttered to the floor.

To another person on another day that would've been it. She was putting herself into an unknown situation. But she wasn't another person.

She was no longer that little girl scared of everyone around her.

She looked again at the door in front of her, almost willing it to be opened. Her jaw was now clenched.

When there was no answer, she tried the handle. To Gina's surprise the door opened up. Country folk often had no use for locks. Ironic, considering the secrets that used to be inside.

The room was dark and stank of stale sweat. It was musty and thick with fear from the ghosts of many children's pasts. She was transformed back to a time when she was a lot smaller. The décor was different then. It had been bad, but now, if it could be possible, it was worse. Things had certainly gone south. The paint choice was now practical, confirming the overheard conversations from her childhood about how the walls showed everything. You'd have to look hard now to spy any bloodstains, but dark brown walls made the place look dark and scary in a way that was probably quite apt.

Her throat felt like it was closing up, and her breath became quick. She was struggling to breathe. It wasn't the smell permeating from the dark and dingy corners but a panic-attack. Something she'd not had in a long time. She held out an arm to steady herself, allowing her shoulder to touch the wall. She remembered the room being a lot smaller. She'd been forced face down on that carpet. She spun around. The room spun. Invisible hands reached out from the shadows and tried to swipe at her. She heard children crying and voices in her head.

"Gina! Why did you leave us!" they pleaded. She was now gasping for breath.

"You saved yourself, but what about us?"

Gina's eyes darted around the room as if looking for faces to match to the voices.

"I couldn't…" she began, unaware she was talking to nobody. "Nobody would've got away!"

"You abandoned us…" a single voice from the dark spoke. It was even, vulnerable and recognisable. "Did you not care for me?" It was Tommy.

"Tommy, no, it was never like that…" The tears had dripped down her face before she even knew she was crying.

"Did I do something wrong?" The voice now choked up and was replaced by the sound of sobbing. That was far worse.

"Tommy?" Gina replied slowly walking towards the dark corner. "Please, Tommy?"

She saw eyes and then something roared and flew at her. She jumped backwards and hit the ground hard.
It wasn't the first time she'd blacked out there.

Chapter Ten

When Gina opened her eyes, she realised where she was and inhaled suddenly. It was like waking up and still being in the nightmare. From the ground she was taken back to the view of the room as a child, looking up at the ceiling and seeing the dark residual blemishes left by the ghosts of those who came before her.

"Where are you all?" she said though unsure whether it was in her head or out loud. The faces that haunted her dreams now seemed so real again. She could picture them all spaced out around the room. Some huddled together, and others thought it was best to hide away on their own. Nobody could consider their tactic much better than anyone else's. They were all beaten eventually. All except one…

The evil lad called Lewis.

Gina got herself up from the floor and wandered from room to room. She was conscious of how long she was there, but she couldn't help it. The last time she was here she couldn't wait to get away, and now she struggled to move and pull herself away from the emotion that strangled her. Despite the years of absence, wherever she turned something else triggered a sick feeling in her stomach.

It was difficult to gauge just how many people lived there now. At one stage there had been five kids. But kids came and went. None of them ever left the boundaries of the property. There had always been three adults: Ma Lyndsey, Ma Vicky and Pa Jeff. Each one was as mean as the other. Often, you'd expect to find a weak link. Here you had to go somewhere else for that. Of all of the bones in the three of their bodies, not one of them was good.

This was a house, but even now it didn't seem much like a home. The place was in need of love – or if nothing else, a damn good cleaning and an exorcism.

Gina never expected the emotion that overwhelmed her. Twin lines of tears cascaded down her cheeks, and for a minute she sobbed uncontrollably. The tears were for herself and for the kids that she'd known, but mostly for the kids still trapped here. The ones that never made it out alive. She knew she'd been naïve to think she wouldn't be affected by it and momentarily wondered whether she might suddenly be paralysed to the spot.

There were photos of the adults grinning like arseholes whilst the children looked forlorn, accepting their lives as the best of a bad situation. With a quick movement she whipped out one of the photos and stuffed it in her jacket. It was Lewis, now a fully-grown man; his picture was placed proudly there on the mantelpiece. He was grinning from ear-to-ear and standing next to a scared boy. He was a teen but only just.

Tommy. A black eye there for the world to see.

Jeff was seen in another photo, equally amused and enjoying life, just like she remembered from the shop earlier. His hand was on the breast of Ma Vicky who was laughing. She was skinny and might've been attractive had she had teeth and appreciated hygiene. She wore a vest, and her bones were prominent. Ma Lyndsey was a large lady who had smudged red lipstick to make her stand out. Her bulk stood next to them with an air of jealousy on her face. It was easy to see which wife was the favourite. Gina had once had the misfortune of looking in on them when the three were naked and grunting. Ma Lyndsey had certainly been dominating the smaller woman then and slapping her hard. It had not been a pleasant sight and looked more like they were all fighting than showing any sort of tender intimacy. The larger lady was American and came over from Tennessee. Her voice came out as a whine, and she liked to verbally put everyone else down.

She stopped at the master bedroom. The sights that she'd seen there were tattooed across her brain. She'd been assigned as the lookout. When the adults were in there fooling around together, Lewis would get the kids to do things like sneaking out snacks (if they were lucky), or sometimes he'd tried to replicate what he saw happening in the room (if they were unlucky). It would've been the perfect time for them to escape but of course they never could. Lewis would stop them. He was in charge of them, and in Gina's eyes the lad who was only a year or two her senior was what stood between her and freedom.

Except he was different, and she knew that because she had been the same.

She turned away from the room. She'd seen too much. Only years later had she learned that what she'd seen wasn't considered normal, but that should not have surprised her. Nothing that happened in this house could ever be described as normal.

Gina walked around the rest of the rooms. The place was empty. She hoped they no longer fostered children. Maybe the authorities had finally caught up with them. Relieved, she walked out of the unlocked backdoor and looked down the garden.

She stopped in her tracks. The ominous shed sat lonely away from the house. The small wooden building cast evil from its pores, a reminder of everything wrong with the world. A prison cell they'd all been sentenced to for great periods of their time here.

She almost felt it grin at her, welcoming her back.

Walking towards it she was again taken back to the times when she had been dragged by her arms and legs along the dusty pathway. She had cried and screamed many times along this trip, limbs burning with pain. The more noise she made, the tighter the grip on her wrists. She soon sucked it up and muffled her pain. They all enjoyed her vocalised displeasure far too much.

Today though she remained quiet for the first time ever. She was in complete control of her body as she willingly walked towards it.

Jim Ody

It was with a morbid fascination that she wanted to see it closer. The smell of the shed hit her as she got near, triggering more deep emotions. Musty and old but with the smell of a man's spilled seed soaked into the wood. The structure was held together by the broken souls of many children. Many, she guessed, were buried not that far away from where she stood.

She circled it once. She stopped and looked out behind it. There was a line of mounds going off away. Most had grass now grown over the top of them. No proper attempt to hide them and what they represented. She knew that each marked the final resting place for a child who never got out even though there was nothing to confirm that. Disrespected in life and death. Each child abandoned by their parents, abused and then rejected by foster parents. Life never showed any interest in them and any higher power was happy to turn the other cheek. Lost in the system they slipped from society and were laid to rest as an afterthought away from everyone else.

Far off at the end was one without grass. It looked like it had only been filled that day. The shovel stood erect like a makeshift gravestone.

With more tears, she looked back at how innocent the outside of the shed was and how badly she'd been treated inside. That small area held everything that was ever bad around here.

She needed to see inside.

The door had a padlock on it. Defeated, she picked it up with frustration. She squeezed it gently at first and then a bit harder. She knew it was a pointless act, but she needed it open. Everything deep inside of her

Sweet Vigilante

willed it to open. It was stupid, she knew, but she did it anyway.

The click sound shocked her but not as much as when the lock opened. She couldn't explain it.

Without any thought she chucked it down and opened up the door.

The horror of the place smacked her hard. It looked exactly the same. Scratches on the walls made by her. The smell was horrendous. She didn't want to go in any farther.

And then she saw the scared little girl huddled in the corner, covering her face with her knees as if that would save her.

Instantly, the child made a petrified sound too scared to control herself, the anticipation of more pain was too much for her. The small body did it's best to try and camouflage into the background. The muddy clothes might've helped had they not once been white. To see a child reduced to this was heart-breaking. But it wasn't just that. It was how she looked when she finally looked up with pleading eyes.

The exact same way Gina had done years before.

Chapter Eleven

The child was petrified. A picture of neglect unable to communicate. Gina knew all too well what that felt like. She couldn't believe that people were capable of this. In the years since she'd escaped, she'd slowly come to realise that this wasn't the norm, and in general people were kind to each other.

Gina tried to smile reassuringly at her, but from experience she knew it would take more than that to earn the girl's trust.

"I'm not going to hurt you," Gina said, holding out her hands defensively. "I'm here to help you."

The girl was about eight years old and dressed in a dirty white blouse and denim shorts. She had matted blonde hair that with a wash and comb would still be beautiful again. Her eyes were silently pleading, and Gina knew they had already seen things no child should ever have to.

"You can trust me. Please. I want to get you away from here."

Sweet Vigilante

The girl made a move but stopped. She was clearly weighing up her options. It was a shame that she would even contemplate staying where she was to be the better option. It was how they were able to do this. The fear of the unknown was deemed worse. A cult-like usage of psychological mind games.

"Quick! Before they come back," Gina smiled in a soft calm voice. "I want to get you to a better and safer place."

The girl looked around herself again although they both knew there wasn't much to see, nor was there anything to stay for. She shuffled over, not wanting to look Gina in the eyes. Gina held out her right hand. The girl looked suspiciously at it but eventually placed her tiny hand into Gina's. A small token of trust.

"Let's go," Gina said. "We're going to make a run for it, okay? My car is down the road. We'll run to it and you will never have to come back here again, deal?"

The little girl looked up with her green eyes and nodded. A child wanting to believe so badly, but one who had been let down many times by adults before. Just for a second there was a slight twitch of her mouth as a wave of optimism moved around her brain. She almost smiled, but her mind didn't fully allow it.

They tried to jog around to the side of the house, but the girl, weak and malnourished, found the physical exertion too much. Gina felt her anchor them back.

"I know it's hard," she said to her, bending down. "But we have to get out of here."

Then there was the sound of a motor, and the car turned into the drive.

Jim Ody

"Stay still, sweetie," Gina said, peeking around the side of the house. She saw three people in the car. She glanced back to see the little girl looking petrified.

"You're safe with me," she said softly, and then turned back to the people.

They were older and life had hit them all hard, but Gina recognised each and every one of them. She wished she had a gun and three bullets. For most of her life her wishes had always gone unanswered.

She saw them talking, and as they got out the words became audible.

"They need to move that pile of shit from the road! This ain't no fuckin' car park!" The guy from the bookstore said as he got out of the car. He tugged at the back of his jeans. A thickset woman with badly dyed blonde hair heaved herself out of the other side. She itched at a point on her leggings, and large braless breasts tumbled around under her vest with each movement. It was like they wanted to break free. The skinny woman patted Jeff's backside as she trotted by. She wore denim shorts and a bright pink bikini top. From a distance she looked vaguely attractive. Time had been kinder to her.

"I need a back rub," Jeff said as they disappeared out of view towards the house. A deep laugh from Lyndsey barked out like a walrus as the sound of the door opening could be heard.

"I'll give ya more than that!" Her voice could be heard before the door was slammed shut.

The little girl was holding on to Gina's hand for dear life. Her little fingers gripped her hand as hard as she could.

Sweet Vigilante

"Let's go!" Gina whispered. She felt the adrenaline flowing through her veins as they sprinted down the drive. It felt such a long way, and she wasn't sure the girl could make it. The mud seemed to slow them both down, and they had to be careful not to slip. Gina felt the weight pulling again as the girl struggled.

"Just a bit further!" They got to the gateway and towards the freedom of the road.

"Don't look back! That's my car over there. Get in!"

Gina opened the door and got the girl in before running around to the driver's side. She jumped in and turned the key to the ignition. The starter motor clicked a bit, and just as she was about to panic, it kicked into life.

From somewhere a gun went off with an almighty *BOOM!*

She saw the guy standing still with a big shotgun. That was always the problem with country folk. Somehow, they were able to get their hands on guns and argue they were for pest-control. She'd forgotten about his gun. It had been unloaded and mostly for show. Shotguns are notoriously slow to load, aim, and fire unless you're an expert. It bought her time as she saw him fiddling with the open single-barrel.

With a screech of tyres, she stood on the accelerator with all her weight like it would aid the getaway further, and they shot off like a Formula One car at the beginning of a Grand Prix – albeit heading the wrong way. She'd find another way to get back to the city. She just needed to put some distance between them and the house.

Jim Ody

The relief was a complete rush. She glanced in her rear view mirror to see Jeff running out into the road waving the gun rather than aiming it.

For the second time in her life, she'd escaped that hell house. Her heart was still pounding in her chest.

"You okay?" she asked when they got a mile further down the road. She smiled looking over at the girl.

The girl nodded. She looked to be in utter shock. Tears began to run down her cheeks. Gina hoped to god they were tears of joy.

"Don't cry, sweetie. You're safe now. You never have to see them again."

The little girl reached over and tapped Gina on the knee. "Thank you," she said in a small frightened voice.

"You're welcome, sweetie. You're so welcome." It was all Gina could do to not well up, and for the next few miles they drove and cried together. Gina continually glanced in the mirror to see if they were being followed. Her adrenaline was still rushing through her veins. Eventually they were both smiling. Gina began to relax.

"What's your name?" Gina asked her when she felt they were comfortable.

"Cornelia. If it's easier you can call me Corn, or Lia," she said in a voice that had grown with confidence, but still she looked down unsure of what Gina's reaction would be.

"What would you prefer?"

The girl shrugged. "They never called me by my name, maybe they forgot it."

"Okay, I'll call you Lia then. How would that be?"

Sweet Vigilante

"I'd like that," she smiled. "I'd like that a lot."
"Well, Lia, are you hungry?"
Lia nodded and smiled.
"Let's stop and get something then, huh?"

Again, the girl looked happy and excited. Gina wondered how long it had been since Lia had felt that way. She knew herself that she had never felt happy in that place. The best side of happiness she ever got was either when something bad was over, when she got some food that looked and tasted alright, or when she dreamed. Indeed, perhaps her only happiness was far away in her sleep.

Within ten minutes, the country roads had turned into towns. Gina welcomed the other cars and people.

They pulled into the carpark of a popular fast-food restaurant. Gina got out of the car, but Lia hesitated. Her eyes darted left and right. The fear had returned.

"It's okay," Gina reassured her. "We'll be surrounded by other people. Even if they did find you, there is no way I'd allow them to take you back. I promise!"

Lia nodded, and slowly she got out of the car and trotted around the front of the vehicle, whilst all the while her eyes darted everywhere. She grabbed Gina's hand and looked a little more relieved.

Gina smiled down at the child. Her heart was already swelling, and she began to understand what it might be like to have a child of her own.

It wasn't long before they were munching down cheese-burgers and drinking colas. The familiar and banal normality of the place was strangely comforting.

Lia didn't talk much. At first, she eyed the food suspiciously, but when encouraged, she set about it like she'd not eaten in days. Gina didn't push her to talk as they concentrated on their food. She knew the girl had been subjected to a strict regime, and so she gave her as much rope as she could. When Lia had finished, she pushed aside the remaining fries and her face suddenly dropped. It was like the life had dropped out of her.

When she spoke, her words were sodden in worry. Her voice was small as she asked, "Are you going to take me back now?" she asked with fear in her eyes. "I mean, thank you for the trip…"

Gina put down the last bit of her burger. "Oh, sweetie. God no. You are never going back there again."

Lia smiled at that. "Thank you," she said again in a small voice. "Are you an angel?"

Gina's face lit up, and she felt her throat constrict with sadness. "No," she replied, shaking her head. "Far from it. I just had to come and find you…"

"That's what an angel does," she replied matter-of-factly. "Save people." Gina had no response, she was right. The words lost themselves in her mind for a while and really made her think.

The girl smiled again. For the first time she seemed to drink in her surroundings. The popular fast-food chain was boringly mundane to most of the patrons there, but to Lia, this was all new. The bright colours were a contrast to the dried-blood brown walls of the house.

"Do you know how long you've been there?" Gina asked. "At the house, I mean?" She knew it was always going to be hard to deal with time since Lia was so young. Even a week would seem like a lifetime to her.

She shrugged. "A few weeks, I guess." She then went quiet.

She took a slurp of her drink and then said. "I don't have any family. They all died when I was little. I was in some intoosion."

"Institution?" Gina corrected, amazed at how this child now rattled off a conversation with ease.

"Yeah, there, then them people came and got me. I thought they was my new family." Her head dropped almost in shame. "They were really mean!"

"Oh, sweetie, that is just awful."

An older couple caught her eye and smiled. They were too far away to hear their conversation but close enough to see how cute the woman and girl looked together. Gina liked the fact the people would think Lia was hers.

Gina finished her burger, all the while thinking about what she should do.

She knew what she should do. She should go to the police – that was an obvious thing to do. But what would that achieve? There was no evidence of any wrong-doing, and Gina could see it now how they would play it out like she had locked herself outside. They would have crocodile tears running down their faces and be full of surprise at these allegations. "We love her!" they'd cry. Then they'd accuse Gina of kidnap. Nothing good would come of it. Nothing at all.

Gina thought back to when she was young and the things that had happened to her. She had no desire to relive those horrors. She was no longer a victim. She was now in full control of her life and she refused to be one again.

She knew what she had to do.

If Lia was passed back into the care of the authorities, then she ran the risk of it happening again. She refused to put Lia back in that position. She would not allow a victim to be lost in the system again.

At the age of twenty, Gina decided to become a mother; one of the furthest things from her mind that morning. Lia would be looked after until she was old enough to look after herself.

"What if you stayed with me for a while?" Gina said, looking into her coffee. On some level she was scared of the possible rejection. It was amazing the amount of times an abused person stayed where they were, blinkered into assuming anything else would be worse. They held on to a thin thread of nostalgia, building it up into something it never was and believing that there was no reason they could turn their back on that.

Lia looked wide-eyed back at her like she'd just been offered a puppy. "Really?"

Gina nodded. "Really. I could be like your mum." She instantly regretted adding the last bit, but it had just slipped out. "You know, if you want, that is?"

"Wow!" Lia seemed so happy, and Gina wondered when the last time was that she'd felt that way.

And that was that.

Without the conception, the discomfort of being pregnant, the antenatal visits, doctors' appointments, hormone changes, cravings, body-changing, physical exertion, and of course the actual birth, Gina became a mother.

Just like that.

Chapter Twelve

Five years ago

It wasn't so much a strength she possessed as grit and determination. She couldn't take it anymore. She'd seen what happened to children who stood up to them. The pain was inflicted with pure pleasure until one by one they were taken away never to return. It wasn't even a Darwinian natural selection. If Jeff or one of his women took a dislike to someone, then their cards were marked. Slowly they would be mentally and physically beaten down until they were told their attitude had been unacceptable and a new family had been found for them. Some of the younger ones saw this as hope. They thought they could play up and they too could be placed with new foster parents, but the older kids knew exactly what that meant. A child with black eyes would not be granted any reprieve. They would be silenced, and that meant their new home was

Sweet Vigilante

not with a smiling family in suburbia but in a dark hole way out behind the shed.

Sometimes days would be long hours of boredom. A break from pain, from being belittled, or worse being touched by an adult that should know better. Then one day, inside her confused mind, Gina had discovered a room. When things were bad and she thought she couldn't carry on, she'd open the door to that room and walk inside. All around her were pretty things. All soft and feathery. Nothing there could do her any harm. She'd pick up each item and brush it gently against her cheek. She loved it there. No horrible men came to her. No foreign objects were inserted into forbidden places. No lies were told. No threats for telling. Numbly, she stayed there, blocking out reality for as long as possible. She would walk out the door to a white sandy beach, she'd turn to an ice-cream van and grab the biggest cones of large white swirling goodness covered in nuts and chocolate sauce. She'd had one once and it seemed the most wondrous thing in the world! When she looked around, she saw other new children, but everyone was smiling and there was no sign of bruises or cuts and scrapes at all. Then when she'd had enough, she'd wave to her friends, make plans to do it again before walking back into her room, slipping into her large soft bed and falling into a deep sleep.

She'd wake up with a smile on her face, curled either in the attic, or with her face using a mound of dirt as a pillow as she lay huddled on her side in the shed.

Then one day, whilst she was once again banished to the shed, she realised something.

Something that would change her life forever.

The shed was not a strong structure like the house. It was built from wood and nailed down. The door was locked, but the floor had begun to rot away. Sometimes at night wild animals would scratch at the outside of the shed determined to get the prize inside. As an assortment of fluids had soaked through, the smell was what attracted the animals. However, with time on her hands, she was able to prise up a couple of boards.

The shed was laid on railway sleepers. There were no deep footings like the house. At one end, there was a small glimpse of light. It was on this light that Gina hung her hope, as night after night she dug under the space towards the gap. A hint at her freedom. So near and yet so far.

By morning, she'd replace the board again. With a resigned disappointment, she would be dragged back to the others, the chance of escape dashed from her until the next time.

Thankfully for her, the older lad, Lewis, had taken an instant dislike to her. Lewis, for the most part stayed with the kids, but he also got to go out on trips. There was no doubt about it, he was the favourite. Jeff saw him as a son. Maybe he was, who knew? Gina didn't think he'd be treated any differently if he was.

He liked to tease her. "The next time you're taken by him, I'm coming, too!" He grinned and licked his lips. His features sneered. He was like a snake. He sat in the shadows with eyes that leered and trousers that tightened at the sight of anxiety. His only way of keeping his own fear away was to inflict it on others.

Sweet Vigilante

"He wouldn't take you, too," Gina had replied matter-of-factly. She hated him right back. She wanted to hurt him badly but always struggled to maintain any sort of eye contact with him, and he knew it.

"Why not? He said I could try, too!" his eyes glanced down to her body. She'd developed breasts a while back, and she could tell Lewis was desperate to get his hands on them. He was a teenage male with no moral compass. He grabbed what he wanted and struggled with understanding right from wrong. If he wanted to get his hands on her, Gina knew it was only a matter of time before he would.

"Get lost," she hissed at him, a feeble defence that worked in the same way you might threaten a bear with a feather.

He grinned like the devil. "I'm looking forward to it! I've thought about it for a very long time. I think deep down, you've been thinking about it too."

She swung an arm, but it hit nothing. It was more like swatting a fly and missing. But somehow, a mug from the side flew off and hit Lewis in the side of the head. The surprise of it knocked him off balance. He sat there, unconsciously rubbing the side of his head and stared at her. There was something that changed in his face. It was surprise with a knowing recognition.

"Interesting," he grinned.

The quick thud of footsteps told her she would be removed from the room. Her arms burst with pain as she was dragged down the stairs and, eventually all the way out to the shed. Looking back, Lewis was smirking at her, but that wasn't it. He was used to her being dragged away. Something between them had changed, and she thought they'd both sensed it.

Jim Ody

A laughing cackle could be heard shattering the quiet night as the door was locked and she was left with nothing but her thoughts.

She took no time in using the water bowl to scoop out more earth. She worked hard and methodically.

And then she heard whistling coming from outside.

Frozen, she stopped. She heard the footsteps get louder at the same time as she heard the voice say her name in a sing-song way, "Gi-na! Gi-na!"

As quickly and as quietly as possible, she replaced the boards. She scattered out the dirt into the corner. She moved back slowly against the far wall as the voice sang out her name again. This time the sound moved around the outside, taunting her.

But this was not Jeff, nor either of his wives. It was Lewis.

"Poor little girl, without a family," he added mock crying. *"Please help me. Nobody wants me. Nobody loves me!"*

She felt anger build up inside of her. She wanted to stand up and run at the door. Smash the wood apart and attack him in a bad way.

But then he was rattling the lock on the door. He was making a horrible chuckling sound.

Maybe he was going to let her out, she thought.

When the door swung open, he was silhouetted by the moonlight. His hands rubbed against the sides of both legs. He looked to have nothing other than setting her free on his mind.

"And there she is," words slid from a mouth that only knew evil. "Poor innocent, Gina."

Sweet Vigilante

"What do you want?" The words almost stuck in her throat, and when they finally formed, they held no conviction.

He laughed to mock her. "I know you're not naïve, Gina. So, let's cut the crap."

"Why are you doing this? Don't you want to be free? You think they love you, but you're just as much a prisoner as I am."

He shook his head. He wasn't having any of it. "That's not true. You can believe that if you think it makes you feel better, but I get taken out to places all the time."

"But you're not free," she added again. Inside, her mind was flicking through scenarios.

"I'm as free as I need to be." He stepped closer. He held a bat in his hand. She glanced down at his feet. The old trainers caked in dirt. He thought he was special – and against her, maybe he was – but he was still a prisoner, whether or not he wished to acknowledge it.

"The funny thing is you are free, but you just don't realise it yet." He spoke in a way that sounded condescending but she wondered.

"I'm hardly free," she managed.

He grinned. "You stupid girl. You have everything you need but the brains to do it. I *could* kill you here and now. That would certainly set you free, but that's not what I'm looking to do. That's not fun to me. I want you to *know* what you can do, and then that's when the fun will really start!" She had no idea what he was talking about.

She felt the anger build up and concentrated on his steps. Almost counting them.

That's when he tripped. His arms flung out to soften the fall. The bat dropped from his grip.

As it bounced, her hand scooped it up as she sprung to her feet. She turned and swung the bat hard as he looked in horror. His arms unable to come up in time to protect him, the bat made a loud thud against the side of his head.

His body went limp.

Still holding the bat, she ran out of the shed like it was on fire. With one last look back behind her, she pumped arms and legs and ran with everything she had.

At the road, her lungs were burning. She no longer had the opportunity for exercise. She'd become weak and unfit.

The road scared her. She could imagine the adults' car finding her quickly. Instead, at the first opportunity, she scrambled over a gate into a field and ran diagonally away. She figured they'd naturally assume she'd follow the road. Any person lost, looking to find civilisation would, but in a survival situation the cover of darkness, coupled with trees and bushes, provided her the natural camouflage to escape and remain hidden.

It was a long night. She did her best to keep moving. She tripped and fell a number of times, but as night turned into day, large buildings started to become visible in the distance, and from there she hoped she'd made it.

Of course, she also knew this was just the beginning. She'd swapped one horror for another, and she wondered how she was to survive living on the streets.

All of the time she thought about what Lewis had said and finally understood. He'd not come there to kill her. He'd not even come to molest or attack her. He wanted her to realise that she was like him. That they had some strange connection. He knew she'd attack him. He had been there to set her free.

It was a game and at some stage he'd try to find her.

Chapter Thirteen

After the meal, Gina and Lia sat back in the car and they headed back towards the city.

"We're just going to go to the hospital," Gina said. "My pops is there. He got sick and they are looking after him."

"Your pops?"

Gina nodded. "Yeah, he's like my granddad."

"Oh," she looked sad. "I've never had a granddad. I mean, I probably have but I don't know him." She was such a sad little girl.

On the way to the hospital, Gina tried to remain calm. They had fought through traffic to get there, circled the car park a number of times before they found a space, and then pushed past people who congregated outside to fill their lungs with smoke that would put them inside the very same place. All around them people were anxious, either about themselves or friends and relatives.

Sweet Vigilante

A hospital is not a happy place. The smell that permeates is a constant reminder that death is all around. Silent reapers roam the hallways looking for their victims. An opportunist with a permanent grin following the coloured lines on the floors like the hospital underground. They stand over the sick and do everything they can to flatline those unfortunate enough to be staying there.

A young woman glanced up. She was a picture of despair. Her dirty-blonde hair was cut in a way that suggested she cared greatly for her appearance, but now, for whatever sad reason, she'd given up. This was not a look that would make it to her Instagram account. Puffy red eyes bled mascara down perfect cheeks. Maybe she'd post it anyway for sympathy Likes. Social media had gifted the needy with instant gratification. A connection to thousands of strangers with only a fleeting friendship which lay on a bed of half-truths.

An old lady shuffled along the painted lines on the shiny corridor floor. She was focused on where she needed to go and assumed the instructions to follow the lines meant just that. Gina and Lia had to move to the side to let her by. She remained stone-faced, resigned to the news coming her way. The soft whisper of angels surrounded her fading aura. Her walk was one way.

A family smiled as they walked past. Proud parents with a smaller child who was running around. They were the first, and only, signs of happiness so far.

They passed rooms of old people who stared into space. Their bodies were discarded, whilst in their minds they lived out memories from years gone by.

Jim Ody

Others looked ready to pass over to the other side. Hair on end, frail, and a deathly grey colour. It was an awful fact that anyone could end up like this one day.

Within a few minutes, they stood awkwardly in front of Pops. Hospitals never made people look very good. Apparently, they had more pressing matters.

Laid in the bed and wired up to a machine he looked older than she'd ever seen him. The bleeping monitor was not a good fashion accessory for him.

"So, why don't you run that past me again," he said in a whispering voice and smiled warmly. Gina had just finished the story of how she'd now acquired a daughter.

"This is Lia. She was in the house that I escaped from all those years ago."

Pops nodded and then looked over at Lia. She looked worried.

"Hey there," he said to her. "Don't be scared of me. I'm just resting up here. How old are you?" He wasn't used to children and did his very best to soften his tone.

She went to open her mouth and then looked up at Gina. Gina nodded in encouragement.

"It's okay," Gina said. "Remember what I told you? Pops looked after me when I left the house. He's a good guy!"

"Another angel?" she said almost in a bewildered whisper.

Gina nodded. "I think so," she whispered back.

For the first time a flash of colour appeared on Pop's cheeks from Gina's words.

Sweet Vigilante

Lia put her hand on his leg and in a small voice said, "Eight, I think…" And then added, "Did you let her out of the shed, too?"

Pops laughed. "No, I'm afraid I didn't know she was there. I found her wandering the streets a while after she'd run away." It was the best answer for the child that brushed off the reality of what had really happened.

"Okay."

Gina then looked serious. "So, what d'you think? Is this the right thing to do?" She was talking about Lia.

Pops grinned. "In life we have many options. Sometimes the obvious answers are not always the best… Gina, you're a strong woman. I'm so proud of how you have got your life together, and if you think you can look after this pretty little thing, then you have my blessing."

"I'm not being a complete idiot?"

Lia giggled at the word idiot.

"Only if you abandoned her."

"Thank you, Pops…" She said but he could see that her mind was wandering off. He'd seen it before. She was a stubborn woman when she wanted to be, and that was something that would never change.

"Revenge is a dangerous thing, Gina. Always assess the risks, and never take on a task too strong… Think smart." They were just words.

She looked up at him in silence, surprised he knew exactly what she was thinking.

"How…?"

He glanced down at her hand. "I just knew. Look in my wardrobe. There's a safe; the combination is the day I met you."

Jim Ody

"What's inside?" Gina asked, but then another nurse came in. She was short and sturdy and carried a number of medical items on a tray.

She flashed a smile before saying, "Sorry but you're going to have to let Mr Walton rest."

Pops winked at her. "See you soon, little Lia? Stay safe, Gina!"

"Good bye, sir," Lia said with a grin. He'd won her over. He won everyone over.

"Pops. Call me Pops."

"Okay, Pops."

Gina looked back. "I want you back home complaining soon." He raised a weak hand which could've meant a number of things, but at that moment they just felt a love for each other.

"He's nice," Lia said loudly as they walked to the car, and that melted Gina's heart.

"He's more than that, Lia. So much more. He's been like a father to me."

"Like you're a mother to me?" she was quick to add.

Gina nodded. "If I can be the mother to you like he's been the father to me, then you'll be a strong independent woman, Lia!"

She frowned a little. "Is that good?"

"It's very good, Lia! It's the best!"

Gina didn't have a lot of money, but she did have a couple of credit cards with a lot of room to spend. They stopped at an outlet that was situated not that far from the hospital and splurged on a number of things that a girl of her age might require.

Sweet Vigilante

For the rest of the day, they played board games and watched cartoons. This was a world unknown to Gina. One that was simple, stress free, and fun!

Lia was enthusiastic at all of these new things in her life. It could've been so easy for her to curl up into herself, pulling up invisible boundaries to protect her from the cruel world, but Lia wanted to experience these new things. She wanted to hear the instructions to the board games, and the television shows that others may take for granted. She sat with eyes wide open watching everything that was playing out in front of her.

There was no doubt that Lia had been isolated from a normal life but she spoke very well and was quick to learn about the world. She was far from naïve. She was a joy already, and Gina couldn't wait to see what a fine woman she would become.

At one point, Gina just watched her. Lia had a smile on her face while she watched the foolish antics of some cartoon animals that were chasing each other around and trying to hurt each other.

"This is like us," she said at one point. "Like back when there were more children. We'd run around trying to hit one another." It was said in the same way someone might explain they were playing catch.

Lia was a survivor just like her.

Gina wanted to give her everything she never had. And much, much more.

Chapter Fourteen

6 Years ago

It was the last few days of term, and Gina wasn't sure about how she felt about the holidays. Academically, school was easy for her. Each lesson she saw as a challenge, and she loved to learn about new things, but socially she struggled. The place was full of cliques, and not one of them included her. She'd tried hard to fit in when she'd first started. She'd smile and wave at people, but the more she did this the more other kids shied away from her. They became suspicious, and that only made things spiral out of control.

"Hey freak!" The tall, popular girl goaded. "You going back to your witch's coven?" As usual she turned around to get the affirmation of her words from the hangers-on that constantly followed her around. They were already giggling behind hands or waving goodbye to her like she was leaving there and then.

Gina turned to them confrontationally, and the girl recognised the danger. She needed to save face, and her skills in these situations were what kept her in charge of the others.

"Anyway, we don't have time for this. Come on, girls, let's go!" They turned and walked off in unison towards the open door of the classroom.

It slammed shut in front of them. Then in a comical act they all walked into each other. The bully grabbed the door handle and tugged but it wouldn't open.

"What's going on," she muttered, as Gina walked over. They parted and stepped back, a little unsure of her. Gina reached out, grabbed the door handle, and gently pulled it open.

"Perhaps it was just a little stuck," she grinned. The girls eyed her suspiciously and scuttled off like insects to find a dark place to find someone else to annoy.

There was a kerfuffle in the hallway as people gathered around the noticeboard. Next month they were doing a production of *A Midsummer Night's Dream*, and everyone was hopeful for a part. Even Gina. There was an A4 piece of paper that had just been pinned up with everyone's parts listed below. She hung back pretending not to care.

It seemed to take forever, but eventually all the interested girls either grinned and congratulated each other or shrugged and disappeared. She waited for the last to leave and then wandered over. She looked down the cast of characters and the corresponding students next to them but eventually got to the bottom without seeing her name. Everyone who had tried out appeared to have some part in the production, even if it was something made up and without lines. She followed her index finger back down the list.

Her name wasn't there, no matter how many times she tried to find it.

Then from behind came the authoritative voice of Ms Benson, the headmistress.

"Gina, just the person I wanted to see. Can you follow me, please?"

Gina's heart instantly began to boom in her chest. She wondered what the girls had said about her now. She wanted to ask, but Ms Benson didn't take too kindly to backchat. Even innocent sounding questions were construed as being defiant.

"The girls of Hambrook Vale should not need to ask questions of staff. They should only provide answers. We do not permit idle chit-chat, profanities, or any other such vulgarities..." she'd continue for another five minutes or so on the expected etiquette of a Hambrook Vale student, whilst ticking off an endless list of things that were strictly prohibited. Most of which the girls did but in secret. Despite the talk it hardly took a lot of clandestine skills to break any rules, and not one student Gina knew had not broken a handful on a number of occasions.

Perhaps she'd been caught and was being made an example of. That was the sort of thing that interested Ms Benson. The humiliation of a single child appeared to be the learning tool she favoured when hammering home her rules.

They got to the end of the hallway, turned left, and continued up a large staircase that turned back on itself to the next level. From there, and still in complete silence, Ms Benson strode left and to the end toward a large door that bore her name.

She pushed open the door, and the room opened up into a large room with a desk. A scared looking woman sat there behind it, looking like she was waiting to be reprimanded.

"Isabelle, please hold my calls for the next half an hour."

The woman swallowed, nodded, and replied, "Yes, Ms Benson." She then looked at her monitor and pretended to be engaged with whatever was on there.

"Follow me," Ms Benson said, just in case Gina was a little simple and wasn't expecting that. They went into another room that had a huge oak desk with a green leather cover, and banks of books surrounded her, only stopping to show a large window that looked out onto the sports field.

"Take a seat." It was a demand. Gina sat down carefully and felt sick in her stomach.

"Gina," she began. "You have been a pleasant student here at Hambrook Vale. You show great potential, albeit slightly lacking in your application once in a while. However, aside from any minor mishaps, or lacklustre regards for rules, it is with a deep regret that I have to inform you that you will no longer be attending this school at the end of this term."

Gina actually felt her jaw drop open. She panicked, worrying about what it was she'd done to be kicked out, and also what that meant for her, and what her mother would say. She wanted to ask but she was much too polite. Before she could think any further Ms Benson held up a dismissive hand to wave off any thoughts.

Jim Ody

"It's regrettable as none of this is your fault. You see, your mother has failed to keep up with your tuition fees, and despite a number of reminders, she's neither returning our calls nor answering any correspondence." She shook her head and actually made an effort at looking as regretful as she suggested. She then leant forward, clasping her hands together and eventually having them come to rest with her fingertips touching, and continued, "We cannot continue like this, I'm sure you can understand. We are a prestigious school with great history. If we are seen to be an easy touch then we'll have any Tom, Dick, or Harry here." Gina didn't want to say that as it was a girl's school that was highly unlikely. A couple of terms ago a student had been removed when it was discovered she was bisexual. It was a silent rule that sexuality could only be heterosexual and by no means could be practised nor explored further.

"Unfortunately, at the end of this week you will be leaving for good. Have you got anything you'd like to say?" Gina was caught on the hop a bit, but really what could she say?

"No, Ms Benson," was all she had.

"Very well then, please use any spare time to pack your things together."

That was that. The extent of her time at the all girls school.

That Friday when everyone left, the only person sitting cross-legged on the gravel and surrounded by her belongings was Gina. Her mother didn't turn up.

As the sun came down Isabelle was called back to take Gina home. It wasn't an act of kindness but a way to finally wash their hands of her.

Isabelle didn't say a word for the whole of the journey, neither of them wanted to be there, and both wanted it to be over as quickly as possible.

Gina was rejected again.

Chapter Fifteen

When Lia fell asleep to the fourth reading of *The Gruffalo*, Gina just stared at her for ten minutes or so. She wondered how someone could be so horrible to such a sweet little thing. You needed a special type of evil to be cruel to a child. Then Gina wondered how much she was talking about Lia and how much, deep down, she was wondering about herself. She glanced down at the child deep in slumber, oblivious to the world that had changed for the better around her. The way she was still except for her chest that moved slightly along with the soft sounds of her breathing. This was something that she could get used to.

After a time, Gina remembered Pop's wardrobe and the safe, so gently she got off the bed, walked out of the room and along the corridor towards his empty bedroom.

She had never spent much time in his room. She respected his privacy and had no reason to go in there. He was always up early and often late to bed. He spent

Sweet Vigilante

little to no time there at all. He saw the room in a practical way. It was there to change and sleep. He never cared much for being there any other time when he was awake.

The smell of the room was mostly made up of his cologne. She knew he had a haphazard way of spraying it so it landed as much around him as it did on his skin. The mixture of wood and spices was pleasant and familiar. He favoured one brand, and the room would forever smell of it.

It felt strange opening up his wardrobe and seeing clothes she didn't recognise. These were probably from a time before her, and it shocked her to think about how little she knew about his previous life. She wondered whether she had been selfish in how it had always been about her and rarely about him. Another regret to add to a host of them that she was collecting.

At the back was the safe. She pushed the numbers from the day he had saved her, and with a slight tug the door popped open.

There was a gun, gloves, and a belt. These were not items she expected to find in the wardrobe of an old man.

He was giving her his blessing to not just look after Lia but to get revenge for her, at least that's how she took the discovery.

She looked closely at the belt. It was dark brown leather, full of pockets and heavier than it first looked. On closer inspection she saw that the pockets were full. It was some sort of utility belt. She smiled and wondered what the hell he was doing with something like that.

She closed it up and walked out of the room.

Jim Ody

She popped her head in on Lia, but the little girl was still in the same position and fast asleep.

Gina grabbed her phone and sent a text message. Less than three minutes later the door to the flat opened.

Lynne stood there in a plume of cigarette smoke. She'd clearly just finished one, but where she'd put the butt was anyone's guess.

"I thought you were going to tell me the old sod had passed over!" she said.

Gina smiled. She loved this woman like a mother.

"Nah, he's doing okay. I really hope he'll be back in a day or two. There was something else that I wanted to tell you about."

"Sounds ominous. Should I sit down or bring a drink?" Lynne had a tendency to use humour whatever the situation. She also loved to drink. A lot.

"We have wine," Gina said.

"Then why are we standing here chatting?" She winked as she spoke. Gina suspected that Lynne was perhaps a functioning alcoholic. She always had a drink in her hand. *But, did that really matter?* She wondered. She had bundles of cash and no reason to drive anywhere, so in some ways it was a vicious cycle. Without much purpose, she wrote and published more novels which meant she made more money, but was lonely and so drank more. And so on and so forth.

It was only now that Gina wondered whether her constant drinking would be a problem with Pops. He drank a lot more when she was around. He joked that she drove him to it, but they both knew that wasn't the case. He didn't like to admit she had a problem either,

Sweet Vigilante

and so ended up encouraging rather than discouraging her habit. Gina handed her a glass of red wine realising that she was doing exactly the same.

"Let me show you something," Gina said. "Follow me."

She took her into her bedroom, and with a finger on her lips, pointed to the small mound in the bed.

Lynne's eyes widened, and her drawn-on eyebrows raised to the point of almost disappearing under her fringe.

They left the room and headed back to the lounge. There was a lot that needed to be talked about.

"Okay, where did you get that child?" Lynne said, almost exploding the question out. "Did you kidnap her?"

They took their seats, and both had large gulps of wine before Gina continued.

"Has Pops ever told you about how we first met?"

Lynne nodded. "Yeah, he found you on the streets and took you for something to eat. He got the notion that he could change you. I disagreed and thought it a silly idea. I guess I was the idiot." She was very matter-of-fact, but behind it was a lot of warmth she tried to hide.

Gina grinned and nodded at that. "What about before he met me?"

"Girl, you've always been tight-lipped and I've never wanted to pry."

"Lynne, I know the first bit to be true, but you're a writer. Prying is what you do."

"Okay, I've always wanted to ask. *Who wouldn't?* You're a beautiful girl. At first, I was sure you were trying to take all his money, and when I realised that you weren't, I could only imagine what had forced you out onto the streets."

Gina looked at the picture of Pops on the mantelpiece once again. She could never get enough of that picture.

"It was bad, Lynne. I was in a foster home with other kids, and most of us were treated badly. I was locked out in a shed for days on many occasions…" she threw a glance to where Lia was asleep. "Something took me back to that house today. I can't explain it, but I followed my instincts and ended up back there. That little girl in there was locked in the same shed that I had been, all those years ago! I took her… I freed her!"

"So you did kidnap her then!"

"They were the same people who kept me prisoner. They weren't foster parents, they were abusers!"

Lynne's hand had gone to her mouth. She could be quite expressive sometimes. "Jesus, you poor things."

"She has no parents or home. I want to help her like Pops helped me… Do you think I'm being stupid?" But as she said the words, they finally sunk in. She didn't know for sure that the girl had no parents. It's what Lia had told her but more than likely on the back of what she'd been told, too. Again, she needed that validation that what she was doing was right. It was a huge move to make in life, although to her it also seemed so natural. *Why wouldn't you help the child?* she'd asked herself.

"No, you certainly are not. I think that is a wonderful thing."

"I had to tell you."

"You did the right thing."

They sat and talked some more, filling in a number of blanks from each other's pasts. Opening up to Lynne felt so good to Gina, and she hadn't realised just how much she needed it. It was midnight before Lynne left. She agreed to come over the next day and meet Lia. The main reason was because she was going to babysit her when Gina went out.

Gina slipped into bed behind the small child and was prepared to cuddle her until the morning. She understood exactly what it was like to be a mother, which in such a short period of time seemed odd. An invisible bond had built between them, and she felt that it was getting stronger and stronger with every passing moment.

"Welcome home, Lia. Welcome home," she whispered and kissed her cheek.

Before sleep took her, she cried for Lia. And she cried for that other little girl who escaped all those years ago too.

Chapter Sixteen

The light shone through the window like it was coming directly from heaven and landing on the child.

"I thought it was a dream." Lia smiled the next morning as she opened her eyes. Gina grinned at her, sipped her coffee, and put down her book.

"No, this is real!"

Lia pushed herself up onto her elbow and said, "Are you sure I don't have to go back there? I never want to go back. Ever."

Gina hugged her. "No, sweetie, you never have to go back, I promise you! Now, I bet you're hungry, right?"

"I'm super hungry!" she grinned and thrust her hands in the air triumphantly like this was something she wanted the whole world to know. The truth was she was used to not eating for long periods of time.

"Let's get some breakfast then. You want some cereal? Or d'ya wanna go out someplace?"

Sweet Vigilante

"Go out? Like with other people around?" Gina smiled, but Lia's response was so sad. It would be a while before she could get used to how free she was now.

"Yeah, like for pancakes at Max's or something?" Gina had no idea what the little girl would like, and at this stage she just wanted to make her happy. She knew soon she'd have to set down rules and boundaries. But Lia had been through so much and she needed her to see that freedom, and that most people were kind.

"Yes please!" She again pumped her hands high.

Gina helped her get changed into the new clothes they'd bought the day before. Gina knew she really needed to buy some food, and more to the point she needed to learn how to cook! That could be the biggest challenge. Going out was fun but it was expensive, not to mention giving the wrong impression on how a person should live.

She grabbed her phone and tapped the name.

"'llo?"

"Baxter? It's Gina."

"Hey, Gina, how's Pops doin'?"

She smiled, and it was good to hear his voice, even if their friendship was purely platonic. She felt a pang of guilt as she realised that she should've updated him earlier.

"He's getting there, Bax. Sorry, I should've let you know before –"

"Don't be silly," he cut in. "Sort him and yourself out first."

"Look, can I get a couple of days off? I know it's short notice, but something's come up. I'll fill you in when I'm back. Is that okay?" The words flew out of her mouth at machinegun pace.

"He hot?"

"Huh?"

"This guy you met? Usually when I get one of these phone calls it's because a member of staff has had too much to drink the night before, ended up with some hot guy or girl, and they want to keep the party going. This usually lasts the day until they fully sober up and realise it was all a huge mistake!"

"A romantic story. No, I should be so lucky!"

"Okay, then. You look after yourself, Gina!"

"You, too!"

"Oh, Gina?" He suddenly said before she cut the call.

"Yeah?"

"Some days I really wish I'd get a call like that from you, you know?"

"What? Letting you down because I'd found a hot guy or girl?"

There was a pause for a beat before he answered. "I think you could do with someone. That's all I'm saying."

"Maybe," was all she said. "Bye, Bax."

"Bye, Gina." She clicked off and looked at Lia who was frowning.

"That was my boss. He's giving me the next couple of days off so we can hang out!"

Lia grinned. "Wow! Cool!" Gina was sure Lia didn't really know what a boss was or what they did, but she quickly picked up the tone of Gina's voice.

Sweet Vigilante

They left the flat and walked down the pavement to *Max it Up*. Set back into the ground floor of a large office building, the diner was a place Gina loved. Gina had known Max since back in the days when she was a street urchin. He'd invited her in a few times and given her free breakfast or a coffee to takeaway. She suspected that he'd been the reason Pops had found her. On occasion they played in a Jazz band together. Tongues got loose after a gig, and laced with whisky they talked about a lost girl. The sadness sobered them up.

Max was a little over fifty and had a shock of tight curly black hair that looked awful when he removed his red cap. Thankfully for him – and most people around – this rarely happened. Max played drums in the Jazz band, and when he did, his red cap was replaced with a pork-pie hat. He thought this was more apt. It covered his hair so it didn't really matter.

"Hey, Max!" Gina called as she walked in.

"Gina, how ya doin'?" he said, grinned, walked out from behind the counter, and threw his arms around her. He was of medium build, but there was something solid about him. Underneath it all was muscle and maybe another story waiting to be told. "I heard about Pops!"

"Who hasn't. The old fool is more popular now than when he was fit. How's things?"

He laughed and then patted his stomach. "Martha says I gotta lose some pounds. She says I'm getting fat… hey, wait a minute! Who's this pretty little thing?"

Gina felt herself swell with pride. She guessed this was something that she'd have to get used to.

"This is Lia. She's staying with me."

"Really? For how long?"

The little girl looked up and smiled sweetly. "Forever!"

Gina and Max both laughed.

"She's right. I'm adopting her," Gina said.

"That right? Well, I dunno which one of you's the luckiest!"

He showed them over to a booth, and they sat down and ordered.

"Martha's right," Gina said to Max when he turned away. He turned back round.

"You think I'm a little rotund, too?"

"I mean you need to watch yourself. Look at Pops. That could happen to you! The two of you should get together and start eating more healthily."

He shrugged. "Well, we could."

"You mean you won't!"

"I mean… I mean…" he sang it as a response that both knew was falling on deaf ears. Men were stubborn. It was programmed into them.

The place was busy. All around people were demolishing platefuls of food. No matter the conversations, or the clientele, you'd see them stop mid-mouthful and nod in appreciation at the food.

Some hair metal band was playing on the radio. The singer was singing about having nothing but a good time, which looking around fit in quite well.

Grease and coffee had never smelt so good. The two went so well together, even if both were considered evil by any dietitian.

Sweet Vigilante

For a little girl, Lia could sure put food away. It wasn't long before she was sitting back with her hands resting on her stomach.

"Full up?" Gina asked.

Lia nodded. "I think I might pop!"

They had talked constantly through the meal. Gina was enjoying thinking about the world from a child's point of view. It was something that she'd never done before. She was also surprised at just how much an eight-year-old knew about the world and how she was able to take everything in her stride. This was something to be thankful for, Gina thought. Lia may get away with growing up with little sign of what she had been through, unlike herself who was plagued by nightmares.

And then it hit her. Last night was the first time in a long time that she'd not had nightmares or flash-backs. It only reinforced her decision to take on this child as her own. They would both get something out of the relationship.

They grabbed some books and toys from the shopping centre and headed back to the flat. Lia was a bright child, but her reading was poor. She was at that age where she'd needed encouragement to read, and this had not happened.

"Have you been to school?" Gina asked her after the first time they'd sat down to read. Although from her own experiences she knew the answer.

Lia shook her head. "I went to a place with other children a couple of times, but then they stopped taking me. They said I was bad."

"The place in the village?"

Lia nodded. "Did you go there, too?"

"Yes. Like you, only a couple of times. They didn't trust us not to say anything." Lia definitely found the transition easier knowing that Gina had been through it all, too.

If their lives had been so different, Gina wondered, *would Lia have not stayed with her, run away at the first opportunity, or asked to go to the police?* She was sure this was the case.

But that evil place did one single good thing. It bonded them.

Every time she looked at that sweet face she was hit by visions of the squalor where she had been living. But it was the memory of her huddled in the corner that sent the deepest pain into her. Not just for the poor girl, but for the other one. The one that grew up and stared back at her in the mirror.

She couldn't shake the feeling inside. Pops had known what she was thinking. Perhaps if she'd been brought up from an early age with the right values then she would not have these thoughts. She had at least had an education, but even that they had not seen fit to bother with. They were evil people. They could not be allowed to do this again.

When Lynne popped over, Lia went slightly into her own shell, but that was only to be expected.

"Hey, sweet thing," Lynne said, sipping another glass of wine. "You don't have to be scared of me!"

"Lynne's a writer, Lia. She writes books and sells thousands all over the world!" Gina said in the over-excited way that kids respond to.

"Really?" Lia said, now looking at Lynne. "What, in America, too?"

Lynne laughed. "Yes, even in America!"

"Has the President read your books?"

Lynne shrugged. "Who knows? Maybe."

"Wow! That's cool!" she grinned.

That was all it took. They sat and played some card games for a while. Gina was pleasantly surprised at how much Lynne seemed to enjoy herself playing with Lia. It then occurred to her that perhaps it had been years since she'd had the opportunity.

It was only when Lia popped out to the toilet that Lynne was able to speak about her.

"She's a cute little thing, Gina," she said in a whisper.

Gina nodded, and beamed back. "This is so strange, but I'm having more fun than I've had in years. I just wish Pops was here to enjoy it, too."

Lynne nodded. "I agree. You know what else? I've hardly touched my wine. That little cutie-pie has made me forget about one of my most favourite things!"

They laughed, and then Gina quickly asked her, "Lynne, can you come over tonight and look after Lia? I need to go out."

Lynne paused and threw a glance at the bathroom. "You're going out? It's the child's second night, and you're going out to bed a man?"

Gina rolled her eyes. "God, no! Nothing like that. It's something I have to do. If it's a problem –"

"It's no problem. Of course, I'll be here… are you sure about this? Whatever it is feels like some knee-jerk reaction."

"Sure about what?" Gina tried to look confused but they both knew.

"You and Pops are more similar than you realise."

Lia came skipping back into the room.

"Just be very careful," Lynne said quickly. "Think about everything, and don't let emotions make you take unnecessary risks."

Gina shook her head. "You sound like Pops!"

Lynne laughed. "He knows his sh… stuff!"

"You were going to say a bad word!" Lia giggled.

"Naughty Lynne!" Gina said, and they all laughed.

They played some more, and then Gina put on a movie. Lynne popped across the hall to her flat to get some food. She was determined to cook for them all.

"Lia? D'you like Lynne?"

Lia looked up from the cartoon animals joking around on the telly and nodded. "She's fun!"

"Wonderful. Look, tonight I need to go and see Pops again, so is it alright if she looks after you whilst I'm gone?" Gina hated to lie, but it was the only thing that seemed plausible to a child. We all lie to protect children. White lies and cuddles keep them safe.

Lia looked at the floor and screwed up her mouth in deep thought, but she was suppressing a smile the whole time.

"It will be after you've gone to sleep so you won't even know I'm gone."

"You'll come back?" Lia asked in a small voice.

Gina went over to her and picked her up in a big hug. "Of course I will! We're a team now, kiddo!"

"Then it's okay with me!"

"Thank you." She hated it, but in her mind it was necessary.

Lynne, as it happened, was a great cook. She'd whipped up spaghetti and meatballs which was wolfed down by Lia. The small child again proving that she had a skill for plate-clearing.

"I'm going to be a big, fat cat soon!" she said. "If I keep eating this much!"

"Glad you enjoyed it, Lia!" Lynne said, also transformed by this little spark of life. This was a welcome distraction to her life.

"That really was great, Lynne. I'll have to cook for you one day."

Lynne waved this away. "God, no. I love you, but your cooking sucks!"

Lia giggled behind her hand.

"What?" Gina said pretending to be hurt, and then grinned.

"'fraid so!"

Lia then pointed to Lynne's leg. "Why do you walk funny?"

"Lia, let's not be rude."

Lynne waved it off. "Don't be silly, that's fine." She then rapped her knuckles on her prosthetic leg with a couple of bangs. "It's made of plastic! I lost my old one years ago."

Lia's eyes widened. "You lost it? Like couldn't find it?"

Lynne grinned. "No, child. Not like that. I mean there was an accident where mine was hurt and was removed. The nice doctors made me a new one, but sometimes it's a little uncomfortable after a while."

Lia nodded, accepting the answer before adding. "Was it bad people that did it?"

"It was my own fault, dear. You have to be careful in life."

"Now come on now, Lia. No more questions about Lynne's leg, okay?"

"I don't mind," Lynne said, but Gina threw her a glare. It wasn't a road they wanted to go down.

"Sorry."

"No problem." Everyone was full of smiles again.

It was not long before Lia was yawning. Gina gave her a quick bath, and then they sat down to hear about the mouse in the deep dark woods again. This time it took only one telling before Lia was sound asleep with a smile on her sweet little face.

"This could be good for you," Lynne said with only her second glass of wine of the day.

"You, too!" Gina said, nodding towards the glass.

"Haha. Yes, you could be right. You know me, I'm not the religious type, but this is a gift from someone, you know? This is good for all of us."

They both let the words sink in as they each thought about what this could mean for them.

"I just can't believe it," Gina started. "My life was fine. I was floating along day-to-day in a job I love with people around me. I didn't think I needed anything else, and then…"

Lynne cut in. "You needed more, Gina, trust me. You need a man or woman, but someone to love as a partner. You've found something else in Lia that you cannot get from Pops."

"I feel guilty."

"That's silly. He gets it, believe me. You are a daughter to him. He knows what it's like. A parent can only offer so much, you know?"

Gina shrugged. "I never knew my parents."

Sweet Vigilante

"It doesn't matter, child. You've Pops, and you've got me. We'll always be here. Now you have a daughter and reason to push yourself more."

"But I have responsibilities now?"

"Sure," Lynne said, holding up her hands. "You now have to think of that sweet little thing, but you have your life to lead, too. Don't forget that!"

An hour later, and Lynne had set up her laptop ready to bash out a few thousand words of her new novel. Gina had gone into the wardrobe and retrieved what she needed.

"Lynne? Look, if something happens to me can you look after Lia? Even if you just make sure she has a wonderful family."

"Well now, that's a huge question!"

"I know, I'm sorry."

"Of course, but nothing will happen, will it?"

"I hope not."

Lynne removed the glasses she wore for writing. "You don't have to go through with this, you know that, *right?*"

Gina nodded and grabbed her jacket. "But I couldn't live with myself if I didn't do it."

"Then you must do what your heart tells you to do."

"Thank you, Lynne." They held a glance that spoke a thousand words, and then Gina was gone.

Chapter Seventeen

15 years ago

That first day of her escape was harder than Gina could ever have imagined. She was overwhelmed by everything around her. It was a sensory overload of anxiety and paranoia. Each stranger's stare looked deep inside her soul. She walked quickly amongst the living, searching for something to reinforce her actions to get away. She couldn't believe she was thinking like that. But it was normal to her. A daily routine, which for the most part had structure.

Here she had none. Perhaps that was more terrifying.

She was so scared; a lot more than she could ever imagine. Each person who stared at her filled her with fear. She was sure they knew. She imagined them talking into their phones to Jeff and telling him where she was. She was so paranoid that it became worse to

Sweet Vigilante

think about what could happen to her rather than to live in the moment.

She saw a guy slumped in a doorway, and he called out to her. She turned to see he was grubby, huddled with a sleeping bag, and had a plastic bag stuffed with many things.

"Spare any change?" he demanded through chapped lips and a single dark tooth. At first she was mute. Her tongue had gone AWOL as she struggled to form words, but then her brain kicked in.

"I don't have a penny," she replied and began to cry.

He looked at her with a mixture of pity and empathy, but soon it was enough.

"Where's your parents?" he said, but all the while he looked past her to the potential currency wrapped up in the clothes of those who continued to walk on by.

"I don't have any," she said, wiping tears away with her sleeve and walking off.

"Too bad," was all he said by way of a response. Then he was on to the next person. It was every man for himself when you lived out on the streets. He needed cash, not another mouth to feed.

The day was hard, but the night was harder. She wandered to a fast-food restaurant. At first she stood back too embarrassed to do anything, but soon the smell was too much. She was hungry, and when a family threw away a meal that looked barely touched, she was on it. She grabbed the tray, and holding the nibbled meal, she turned and ran. A woman scoffed at her actions and pulled her child near her for fear of Gina eating him, too. But it was good food to her.

Jim Ody

She'd not tasted anything remotely like it back at the house. And she was desperate.

She sat with her back to a large clothes recycling bin and devoured the food.

Gina wanted to stay away from people. In her experience people were unkind. If anybody helped then it would be for a reason. They always wanted something in return. They'd lead you on purely to hurt you later.

Now she was in the city, and she didn't know where she should go. She tried to stay off the main roads for fear of being picked up by the police. She assumed they'd do nothing but drive her back home, and she'd be in for the beating of her life when they abandoned her.

She walked down alleyways and along dark paths. It was a dangerous route but she knew she had no other choice. The path led to a bridge that had a railway going over the top and a canal by the side of it.

She huddled under the bridge with her back against the wall. The shadows were her blanket, and she wondered how long she would have to stay like that. She even considered this might be where she'd die. More than once she considered that perhaps she was making a huge mistake.

Time moved slowly when you had no place to go. She wondered whether she was counting down her final days on this earth. She just couldn't see how she could survive to get food each day, and when cold winter nights came…

Footsteps broke the silence. The echo was deafening. She gasped and froze. They stopped.

Sweet Vigilante

"What have we got here?" a voice said. It was deep and rasping. Wear and tear on vocal cords from cigarettes or maybe just genes.

She looked up. His face was younger than the voice suggested. He looked like he'd just won the jackpot.

"You working?" he said, his head looking all around. He was licking his lips, cocking his head to the side, and speaking with a half-grin. She amused him.

Gina didn't know how to respond. "I have no money," she said. The words slipped out before she could pull them back. She knew it wasn't the right thing to say. In fact, it was the complete opposite of what she should say, but she was clueless to her dire situation.

He nodded and fumbled in his pockets. He produced a bank note. She couldn't tell how much it was for.

"I got like, seven-quid," he said like he was doing her a favour. "I got a condom." He said it like she should be happy, and he was doing her a favour.

She looked to the ground. A thousand things raced through her head, and before she knew it she'd slowly nodded. He grinned and handed her the cash. She lay back onto the dirt, her eyes glanced up above her. She was used to looking at dirty ceilings in a similar way. She looked at the nests built in the steel girders, as the man fumbled in front of her. His hands quickly pulled down her tracksuit bottoms and knickers.

It was rough, dry, and painful. But soon she became numb to what was happening.

She disappeared through the imaginary door and into her mind. From experience, she knew it would be over soon.

Jim Ody

She pictured a window. Outside was a world of great expectations and wonderful things for her to experience. She looked at the pictures on the wall. The books. She added music. Something nice, slow and soft. A different rhythm from how her body was being forced to rock now.

With one last thrust, she was pulled back to reality. He collapsed on top of her. A blast of rotten breath hit her face as she was squashed by his body weight.

And then his face turned angry.

"What the fuck was that? You were a fucking corpse!" He slapped her, grabbed the money from the ground, and scrambled to his feet.

"Whore!" he shouted and spat in her direction. "You don't deserve anything!"

Stunned, she slowly pulled up her trousers. Overwhelmed by the smell of sex, she sobbed uncontrollably into her raised knees. She'd put up with that for nothing. That money would've bought her a meal, and now she had nothing. She'd thrown away her dignity and had no one to blame but herself.

She wondered whether she'd be able to find her way back home. She wiped away the tears, but fresh ones soon followed.

Had she made a huge mistake? She thought this would be utopia, and instead the world outside of the house was no better.

Chapter Eighteen

The wind was unseasonably cool as Gina got outside her building. Uncharacteristically, she looked both ways, suddenly paranoid. It was interesting because normally when she was out doing her best to protect the city, she didn't care. She slipped out and moved around like a ghost. Now she felt like anything but. She envisaged a large sign above her that proclaimed her intentions for all around to see.

She walked quickly to the car park, scanned it for vandalism, and when satisfied, got inside and sat looking over at her bag. She'd stuffed it with things she thought she might need. She felt the weight of the belt around her, and the baton she'd found in Pop's wardrobe now lay in the footwell.

She didn't have to do this. She could still turn back. She could forget about the whole thing, hug Lia, and focus on giving her the best life possible. That was the sensible option. The thing that most people in her situation would do. Except she wasn't most people and knew if she didn't go through with it then she'd never forgive herself.

She stared straight ahead. Every question was cleared from her mind, lost in thoughts fuelled with revenge. Her muscles stiffened, keeping her on edge.

She didn't have much of a plan. Perhaps she was a little naïve, but she didn't think she needed one. The hate was building up inside her, and the adrenaline pulsating around her body made her feel invincible.

She looked in the mirror. The face staring back at her had a hardened edge. Experience had worn lines into her skin and even deeper into her soul. There was a serious look in her eyes. Perhaps this was what she had been waiting for over the last few years. She needed an outlet, and here it was. Deep down she felt like this was what her life had been building up to.

She started up the car and through memory headed out of the city and towards the house again. It was like she was on autopilot. Her body operated the controls, but her mind was focused on what she would do.

Revenge is a strong emotion and one built on years of abuse. If it's allowed to fester then it is a hell of a dangerous thing.

She stopped at a filling station and got fuel. She had half a tank, but this wasn't just for her car.

She walked into the convenience shop and grabbed an energy drink and a chocolate bar. She nodded to the Asian guy behind the counter who looked thoroughly bored. He was watching a movie on his phone and was almost annoyed she'd interrupted him.

Sweet Vigilante

"That stuff will kill you, you drink too much of it," he preached and nodded at the brightly coloured can of drink. He never broke into a smile.

"Believe me, that is far down the list of things that will kill me," she replied with a wink. He remained stoned-faced and went back to his movie. He didn't like strong women. He liked them even less when they thought they were smart.

She had the can open and had already drained half of it before she was back in her car. She could feel her heart rate increase from the high levels of caffeine and sugar. She felt drugged but alive.

She pulled out and onto the road. The hard-rock band Kiss was kicking ass on her stereo. She banged the steering wheel to the beats of Peter Criss whilst Paul Stanley boasted his sexual exploits to the music.

She was lost in the darkness as the road lights ceased, replaced only with walls of hedges and large trees. The city was a long way behind her when she pulled over to the side of the road. She almost thought about driving right up to the house, but she needed a small element of surprise.

She wanted to wake them up from their sleep the way they had done to her on many occasions, pull them out of their beds half naked and do what the hell she desired.

The night now felt warm as the breeze had dropped. Gina walked purposefully up the driveway noticing that the car was there, even if the house was now in darkness. Her left hand held tightly to a baton.

She walked up to the door and knocked gently. Focused, she waited. The sound of movement was soon heard.

Jim Ody

The door opened, and the large imposing figure looked out.

"Yeah?" he said gruffly, clearly not happy to have been awoken. Gina no longer had her hair up and hardly resembled the girl he'd seen in the bookshop the day before.

Gina then said, "Sorry, but someone was trying to get into your car!"

"What!" he said and stormed out, almost barging into her as he tried to pass.

With a swift movement she hit him with force on the back of the head. He went down hard. She quickly grabbed the plastic ties from her pocket and slipped them around his wrists.

There was more movement from within as the large and familiar lady came wobbling out.

"Jeff? You there?" she said more in annoyance than anything else. She waddled out the door and met the full force of a punch from Gina.

She went down but wasn't knocked out. She turned and looked at the crazy eyes that bore down on her.

"Remember me?" Gina said.

"What? Who are you?" the woman said. Her fat, and braless breasts had almost toppled from her vest.

"I'm Gina, Ma Lyndsey. Gina Chandler."

Recognition exploded in her eyes. "W-what. No. But we loved you… We looked and looked for you!"

Gina kicked her in the side. Her foot was met with little resistance from the fat. It wasn't meant to hurt her but just be annoying.

Sweet Vigilante

"You only loved to hurt me. How many nights did I spend in the shed? How many times did I cry out for help?"

"It was for your own good!" Even now the woman was defiant and standing by her actions. She barely seemed to even be sorry.

"Bullshit! You bitch!"

"Look, I'm sorry. We never did it again after you. We thought…"

"Don't lie to me again or I will shoot you!" Gina's hand hovered over where the gun sat on her belt.

There was some commotion from inside, and Ma Vicky came storming out, topless and full of anger. Gina swung the baton hard and smashed her in the face. The bag of bones crumpled to the ground, crimson appearing through stringy hair.

There was a moaning as the big guy came round.

"How are you, Pa?" she said with a sneer. She felt so good seeing him like that. Bullied, beaten and defeated on the ground. The tables had truly turned. She really wanted to turn him over and force an object inside to see whether he enjoyed it, but she knew how sick these people were and thought there was always a possibility he'd consider it a turn on.

"W-what? Gina, is that you?" He was now feigning happiness.

"You know it's me. You can't hurt me anymore. How many have there been?"

"What?" he said, realising he couldn't move his arms or legs. He tried to hide the panic, but it was there. Men who live for control are the first to panic when they no longer have any. This had stripped him of his power.

"You know! Ma, get him up!" She got to her feet gingerly and walked over to him as Gina pulled out her gun.

She saw them struggle. She cocked the hammer, the sound helping to motivate them to focus and dig deep.

"You taught me about guns. How to use them and how to be scared of them. Funny how that's now come to bite you on the arse, huh?"

They shared glances, but it was obvious to them both that they were in a whole world of shit.

Gina motioned them forward. "Around the side of the house. Now!"

"I can't walk!" Pa shouted.

She looked at him with pure hatred. "Then jump, or I will shoot you!"

It was comical watching the fat lady, in a long dirty vest that hardly covered her large butt, help the large man as he struggled to jump around the side of the house. Gina grabbed Ma Vicky's arms and dragged her. She was all bones so didn't weigh much. It wasn't long before she started making sounds.

"Get up!" Gina shouted. "Or I'll hit you again!"

"What the...? Who are you?"

Gina didn't need to reply as Ma Lyndsey did for her.

"It's Gina, Vi. Little Gina has grown up." She spat out the words, her chubby face screwing up as best it could with contempt.

Ma Vicky turned around and looked at Gina.

"Shit," was all she muttered. She knew she was now in a bad place. Gina had now replaced the baton in her belt with the gun.

Sweet Vigilante

And there in front of them was the shed.

"Down there," she demanded. They stopped and looked at her in horror. They knew that this couldn't possibly end well. Suddenly Ma Vicky tried to make a run for it, but as quick as a flash Gina ran and tripped her.

"Try that again and I will shoot both of your knee caps. Do you know what that feels like?"

The woman shook her head in defeat.

"Worse than when an adult breaks a child's finger, or dislocates their shoulder, or knocks out a tooth. Can you imagine how any of those things might feel?"

Ma Vicky shook her head and got to her feet. Tears were streaming silently down her face. But these were selfish tears. Fear induced.

"The trust that people placed in you. They may not have wanted their children anymore, but they never expected them to be abused!"

Gina turned around to Pa who had already started jumping towards the shed again with Ma Lyndsey.

"What about you two, you fat fucks?"

"They were accidental. You remember it all wrong, Gina!" Pa said. Desperation had crept into his voice, although underneath she could tell, given the opportunity, he would kill her. "You were a child! You don't know what you remember!"

"Shut the fuck up and get into the shed!" Even now he did his best to twist things around and try to confuse her.

They finally got there, exchanged glances, but came up blank. They were worried about what Gina would find. She then realised that despite the rain, and the

Jim Ody

time that had passed, these animals still thought that Lia was in there.

These were evil specimens. They had no reason to live.

"When did you last check on her?" Gina said, and once again the two glanced at each other with worried looks.

"Open it up!" she snapped.

Ma Lyndsey fiddled with the lock, and then slowly opened the door.

She glanced in, expecting a scared little girl.

Of course, it was empty.

"Go in!" Gina shouted.

They walked in slowly as condemned and beaten people. They would never fully understand what their actions over the years had done. The lost children that would never grow up to have normal lives or kids of their own. These awful and evil people had robbed them of everything that life had hoped for them. Gina wanted to go through each child, to spell out who they were and what each of the adults had done to them. She wanted them to be sorry, to plead with her for their lives, but she knew it would do no good. They weren't worth it.

She slammed the door closed behind them and locked it.

"Don't leave us here!" Ma Vicky shouted, and Ma Lyndsey had begun to sob. Gina turned her back and walked away.

They deserved to be left there for days on end, too. They needed to understand the feeling of being neglected and treated like an animal. They had to feel time alone, together. Hours blaming each other. Wondering and waiting.

By morning one of them was bound to be dead. That's what happened when people became desperate. They had to put their time and energy into something. Left to stew, things would be said. Accusations thrown around like wedding confetti. And knowing them as she did, one of them would go too far.

Gina thought about that as she turned her back on them. And walked away to her car.

But more than anything, anger grabbed her. It stuck its ugly face directly into hers injecting her with more adrenaline. Something pushed her on and refused to let her have a conscience.

With a sly grin to herself, she grabbed the red can of petrol and walked back. Her breath quickened as she got closer to the hut.

"Have you learnt your lesson?" she said calmly. Her voice fuelled with the horror of her memories.

"Yes," Ma Vicky shouted back desperately, but Pa refused to speak. "It was all their idea anyways," she added in desperation. The weak ones became obvious first.

"I find that a little hard to believe," Gina replied with a grin. With a twist of a cap, followed by a swing of her arm, arcs of liquid splashed over the shed.

"What was that?" Ma Lyndsey yelped, almost hysterically. Fear slipped its arm around her. Silent whispers tickled her neck.

"That's the sound of hell raining down on you!" Gina said knowing it was dripping inside and on to them, too. The smell of petrol is strong. It races up the nostrils and clogs the back of your throat with fumes.

Jim Ody

"You crazy bitch!" Pa shouted, suddenly enraged.

"I am what you made me," she replied, adding the final line of fuel to the ground.

"Go to hell!" she shouted and fired the gun at the fuel wet on the ground.

It immediately lit up the night and within seconds hit the shed, sending the whole thing up in flames.

She heard the deathly screams pierce the night. But it got to be too much for her and instinctively shot three times through the side of the shed. There were no longer any sounds other than the popping and crackling of the flames eating away the shed.

Satisfied, she walked away. She would've loved to have stayed and watched the building burn to ashes. But glowing flames in the night had a tendency to send distress signals for miles around. She wasn't about to get caught.

She really wanted to stay longer. Roast marshmallows on the heat from their burning skin, but she was too clever for that.

She got to her car and felt no remorse whatsoever. She felt surprisingly good. Having just murdered three people, it might've been considered a strange feeling.

She drove off, giggling with hysteria, away from the house. She didn't meet another vehicle until she was well within the city limits. At that time, most people did their best to keep themselves to themselves.

Back at the block of flats she crept in past the broken CCTV camera and, as quietly as she could up the stairs. She walked into her flat and fell into the arms of Lynne.

"You did it?" The smell of smoke was still strong on her clothes.

Gina nodded. Suddenly she was a mass of emotion. She cried and held tightly to the older woman.

"You smell like Guy Fawkes," Lynne said with a chuckle. Gina sniffed and laughed. "I feel so good about it. That can't be right though, can it?"

Lynne pulled back but still held tight to Gina's shoulders. "What they put you through. What they did to that little angel in there, your actions cannot be seen as anything but a necessity to mankind." Gina wasn't sure, but she needed those words.

"Shower and get to bed. Tomorrow is a new chapter for you."

"Thank you, Lynne."

"You're welcome. Oh, and she didn't stir once."

Gina smiled and headed off to clean away the smell of smoke, petrol, and death from her body.

Chapter Nineteen

Gina felt the day was different when she opened her eyes. She couldn't explain it, but she had slept deeply. Death proved to be a calming experience this time.

She got up and glanced out of her bedroom window. The world was getting on with the things it normally did. The people below with their busy lives rushed against the clock to fulfil expectations. They were animals busy going about their duty, and she felt at ease. The little girl was sound asleep, too.

She knew she still smelt of smoke, so before anything else she stripped off and showered.

The hot water felt great cascading over her, but she washed herself quickly, not wanting Lia to wake up without her being there. She dried herself off and put on some clean clothes before walking into the kitchen to put on some coffee.

She still could not get used to the silence without Pops. The coffee dripped through the filter and into the glass jug in a mesmerising fashion.

Sweet Vigilante

With a mug in her hand, she walked back to her room and looked once again at the sleeping beauty. It was beginning to be one of her new obsessions.

She grabbed her book, and this time she allowed herself to relax and enjoy the story. In fact, it was the sound of her chuckling that woke Lia.

"I thought Aunty Lynne was here?" Lia said as she smiled and stretched.

"Because of the laughing?"

"A little bit." She rubbed her left eye, and then proceeded to do the same with the right.

"She was. We'll see her later."

"Promise?"

"Definitely!"

Lia got changed, and Gina made toast and cereal for their breakfast. Her culinary skills could just about stretch to that. They sat down at the small table and ate, both grinning the whole time. Gina knew that she would have to go back to work the next day, and she also had to start looking for schools for Lia. Lynne was looking forward to babysitting whilst Gina worked. They'd talked about it at great lengths the evening before.

Gina put on the TV. She flicked through the channels until she came to the local news.

It dominated the headlines. A concerned anchor was standing outside the house, clutching a microphone, whilst a mass of activity was happening behind her. Police tape and flashing lights provided the backdrop.

She wasn't surprised to hear the fire was mentioned as being suspicious. The news also talked about a number of mounds found throughout the garden. A number of white tents had been erected, and teams of androgynous figures kitted out in white suits and wearing masks walked about gathering evidence. Gina knew it wouldn't be long until they uncovered the real horror. This was only the tip of the ice-berg of a news story, but one she hoped to stay right out of.

Her heart beat fast. She wasn't sure whether it was the excitement of it all, the relief that it was over, or even the anxiety of making sure she wasn't caught. But never before had she watched the news with so much emotion.

Gina was about to turn it over when she saw that Lia had been watching, too. Her first parenting fail.

"They're dead?" she said, and for a second Gina worried that she was sad about the news.

Gina nodded. "Yes."

"I'm glad," she said. "I know I shouldn't say that, but they were horrible."

"Come here," she grabbed her and held her tight.

"I wonder what happened?" her small voice questioned rhetorically.

Gina didn't need to answer, but she did anyway. "Justice was served, sweetie."

And that was when she saw him on the telly. He was in the background, but prominent enough to be seen. Wearing an expensive suit and grinning like he'd just made his first million.

Lewis.

It had to have been pure coincidence, but for a second the camera did a close up of him just as he turned and looked directly into it. Gina felt an unwanted chill dance up her spine. Right there and standing in a business suit was pure evil.

Sweet Vigilante

Maybe it wasn't all over, Gina wondered, and then the phone rang before she could let it bother her any more. And the news had moved on to something more light-hearted and involved a child grinning and its proud parents overcome with pride.

It was the hospital saying that Pops would be released that afternoon. She couldn't believe it. She was over the moon with happiness. Finally, everything was coming together.

Gina put some cartoons on for Lia as she went into Pop's bedroom and made sure that everything was left as Pops would've expected it to be. The night before had been so overwhelming that she couldn't remember even going in there.

She looked in the safe and made sure everything was back in its rightful place. But she found something that she'd not noticed before.

A scrapbook. Old and full of memories, it had been carefully put together.

She pulled it out and flicked through the pages. There in black and white over many years were headlines and stories cut out and kept by him.

A lone vigilante. A superhero guy-next-door.

This was a guy that helped the poor and needy and brought down the greedy and criminal minded. There were pages of stories, carefully cut and pasted onto each page. He was a normal man without any power other than passion and heroics. The one or two grainy pictures of him were familiar. The way he stood was the same way she'd seen many times before. It was without doubt Pops.

Jim Ody

Gina felt tremendous pride. She thought about how she suddenly had those visions and feelings about the house. She looked down at the ring on her finger.

Who was this ring originally for?

The only thing she knew was that everything had now fallen into place, but it was time to go out into the world and help people. She'd been the lonely and the needy. She'd wanted a superhero to come and set her free. She had to be that person for others. Who else would save them? Sure, she could still serve coffee and sell books, on some level they were important, too, but that was her cover. She was the quiet woman who smiled but didn't say much. Then at night, she would continue to help clean up the city. Just like she'd done for the past few years. Just like Pops.

She looked again at the ring. She could feel the pull to take her somewhere else, but it would have to wait until later.

She still had things to learn about her past, but her future was now filled with purpose.

Legally, she would always be Gina Chandler, but she wondered whether she might one day be dubbed, 'Sweet Vigilante'. She knew she was being silly now, but why not? If she was going to help the police do their job, then why not aspire to having a name.

If nothing else it was another thing that made her smile.

Part 2

Jim Ody

Chapter Twenty

It had been a few weeks since Pops came home from hospital. They'd celebrated with balloons and cake. Lynne had shed some tears which had surprised Gina. She was beginning to think that Pops and Lynne were more than just good friends.

Lia was settling in just fine. She'd started to become quite the cheeky little lady, which only went to prove how comfortable she was with them. Such a character and Pops loved everything about her. The first thing he did was to get Gina to purchase a load more books. He'd sit and read through them with her, sometimes making her read a chapter or two. She picked things up quickly, and had just started attending the local primary school.

Lynne was around a lot more, not that she ever went many days previously without making an appearance, but now she'd even curbed her drinking to only meal times. She'd talked about going further – the whole twelve-steps, but Gina had no cause to push that point. She was doing well with this challenge. Gina

Jim Ody

wondered whether completely cutting off the devil's water would be going too far.

Gina had got back into the rhythm of things at the bookshop. The work and lifestyle balance were just right. Baxter had asked her lots of questions, and of course, she'd mostly lied. In this situation, the truth could only do harm. That night of revenge at the house had to remain a secret. Only Pops and Lynne knew the truth, but even then she was as vague as she could be. They had seen the news stories and read the newspaper articles, so most of it never had to come from her own lips. She even kept it from Abu. Loose lips and all that. Not that she didn't trust him. He was spiritual and preached about karma and forgiveness, neither of which this fell into.

Today Gina was beginning to think long-term. She couldn't help it. Of late, she'd had a new lease of life, no longer just going through the motions. Lia was really good for her, adding perspective and focus. It gave her someone to live for. Previously, she'd just been living day to day, and that had suited her perfectly, but now the words from Pops echoed in her brain about finding someone for her. Lynne had, of course, said the exact same thing.

The first time she saw the guy, she thought nothing of it. Guys often left a lingering look towards her. It's what they did. She didn't mind. She still wasn't in the market for one, but she'd not had a naked tussle in a while. She knew why. She'd not felt the need to dominate a man, to belittle him and make him beg. She knew now it was not about her but about getting revenge on how she'd been treated. To her a lustful man needed to be shown that things would only happen on her terms. No longer would she be the weak woman. She was taking back her life in every aspect.

She'd spent a few nights naked with men where an onlooker would question whether or not they loved or hated each other. She'd scared a few men; others saw it as a challenge. Now she wanted more.

"He's back," Baxter whispered in her ear with a grin as he passed. "I'm sure it's neither the books nor the coffee that keeps him returning. Don't you think?"

Gina shook her head and did her best to gloss over it. She was flattered. And he seemed nicer than a lot of the sleaze-bags that popped in. They were more suggestive, either fascinated by her boobs like they'd never seen a pair before, or overly confident, trying out well-worn lines hoping to make themselves sound cool. Hipsters feigning intelligence in order to let their sociopathic tendencies play out a mating routine seen in one of the recent Hollywood rom-coms.

"Hi," the guy said, walking up to her. He was fiddling with his hands but smiling, looking like he was hiding nerves. She liked that.

"Hello," Gina replied as Baxter scuttled off. The guy had short brown hair with a fringe combed back, and shaved neatly around the sides of his ears. He wore a casual shirt with the sleeves rolled up over strong looking forearms. A tattoo could be seen on one of them.

"Um, do you have any first editions or rarities in a specific section, or are they amongst the others?" At first, she was disappointed that this appeared to be a genuine question. He was nervous, at least that was a bonus. She thought she'd take the lead. She simulated

Jim Ody

a heart attack, her hand over her chest. "Amongst the others!" she grinned. "That would be sacrilegious, would it not? What sort of a book shop would this be?"

He liked that. It calmed him. "I didn't suggest this shop *would*, I was merely asking where I might find them!" He broke into a smile, and she thought it one of the most beautiful things she'd seen.

"Well, you'll find them down at the end of the corridor. That whole section has some great rare titles. Anything in particular you're after?"

He had green eyes. And no wedding band.

He shrugged. "Honestly? No. I like to go buy up any first editions of books I've enjoyed. I'm not a dealer or anything. Just a lover of books. An amateur collector."

"Amateur? What makes a collector that?" He was taken aback by the question like it was a test. Maybe it was.

"A lack of knowledge. I don't buy books because of value, or for investment, but purely because I love to collect rare things."

"Unique," Gina said before she could pull back on the word.

"Yes, or unique."

Gina laughed. "No, I meant *you're* unique! I wasn't criticising your choice of words!"

"Well, I suspect you know more about literature than I do. So anyway, me? Unique?"

"I see many types of people in this line of business. I know all the types. You are a rarity yourself!"

He blushed slightly. "I've only ever been a first edition!" he then looked awkward and quickly added,

"Okay, well I'll see if there's anything down there I fancy."

"You do that. Let me know if you need anything."

He held her gaze for a second. A beat too long. The type that speaks without words. The signal that there is something – however small – happening between them. She was grinning inside but only allowed a polite smile to be shown.

"I will." He flashed another winning smile and walked away. She watched him stride, all the while pretending her eyes weren't lingering on his arse and the way he moved.

Baxter was quick to appear again. He remained silent but threw her a knowing look.

"What?" she said, but it was written all over her face.

"Nothing. You flirt all you want! It might increase your tips."

"I don't get any tips."

"Because you don't normally flirt."

"I wasn't... I mean, I was just –"

Baxter waved off the words. "I'm messing, Gina. I think it's great. You do what makes you happy."

She nodded and found herself twisting her hair like some schoolgirl.

"To be honest, I thought you were gay," he shrugged. "Not that it matters, of course."

"Who says I'm not?"

He nodded, accepting that. "Who says indeed."

Ten minutes later, the guy appeared again with a book in his hand. He waved it like it was a rare treasure.

"I found something."

She grinned back at him. She could tell he was genuinely excited to have found it. That meant a lot. More points to him.

"You did indeed. Deanna Dwyer, *Dance with The Devil*. A good choice. You a fan?"

"Of Koontz? Who isn't, right?"

She nodded. "Who isn't indeed." She rang it up on the till. "And you said you had no knowledge."

He looked at the book. "I know his pen-names as I'm a huge fan. I expect everyone knows the pen names of their favourite authors, right?" He handed over his credit card.

"I doubt it."

She handed it back with the book, and said, "Enjoy it then, Mr Thomas."

He looked at his card, and it clicked how she knew his name. "Noah," he said. "Call me Noah."

"I'm Gina," she replied.

"Nice to meet you," he said. They stood again with an awkwardness before he broke the spell, turned, and then he was gone. He had almost said more. She had willed him to speak more.

She watched him leave the shop and disappear. The sudden sound of books falling brought her out of her daydream. She threw a glance to where it had come from. Baxter was bent over, picking up the books and looking guilty.

"I was willing you kids," he said. When she looked at him blankly, he nodded towards the door. "You know, you and him-with-the-smouldering-gaze."

She rolled her eyes. "When did you turn into Barbara Cartland?"

Sweet Vigilante

"I wish. That woman's a genius!"

It was weird. She couldn't get Noah out of her mind. The worrying thing was it felt like a weakness. To feel as she did towards a man, especially one she hardly knew, felt almost immature. He could have evil pumping through his veins. He might be waiting to get her out and alone before overpowering her and doing whatever he wanted. He might… he might… *he might, what?* She wondered. She knew she had to get out of the habit of being so negative towards men.

And that was another problem. She liked the idea of it. She'd never been like that before. The men of the night who she ripped out from the shadows fell into a submissive character straightaway. They allowed her to take them to wherever she pleased and dominate them.

Again, she didn't want to think any more about what this might mean.

When she took her lunch break, she headed over to see Abu. She felt like she needed some sort of soul cleansing. She wasn't going to ask him for advice, but she'd look at ways she could reconnect herself spiritually.

He only lived a few streets away and it was amazing how within this large city, she frequented only a small area during the day time and perhaps a little further afield at night.

She let herself in the main entrance and wandered down the corridor. She found him sitting in an awkward pose, his eyes closed. But still he said, "Gina. How are you?"

"How d'you know it's me?" She wondered whether he had special powers, or maybe he was actually a god living in a contemporary world.

He gracefully untangled himself like a break-dancer gliding through slow and calculated moves. "For a small woman, you walk like an elephant!"

"What?"

"It's true. You have a lot of inner strength, and that appears to manifest itself in every step you take!" he laughed to himself at that. She felt a little bit offended by the comment.

Gina sat cross-legged on the floor with him. He stared deep inside her. He did this. She assumed this to be his spiritual way, so she never felt self-conscious. It might be on the same level an aged family member might grab the shoulders of a child and study them to see how much they'd changed since they'd last seen them.

"Pops doing okay?" he asked. She nodded. Her gaze floated towards the shrine of Ganesha. The colours popping out around the elephant-like god who sat amongst gold and jewels. Whilst the religious regalia was all around, he rarely spoke of it.

"He's changed his diet. He's trying to remain calmer. He's still trying to get used to plant-based foods."

"He has eaten poorly for so long it's a ritual that must be broken."

"That's what I keep telling him but in a slightly more normal way."

"Demanding, you mean."

"I do."

Abu smiled. "He likes to be busy. He should meditate." He threw his hands up the minute the words left his mouth. "I know, I know. He's not interested in it. I'm saying, it would help!"

"Well, you know what we talked about last time?"

"Nocebo?" A negative psychological outlook on things that can harm the body when positivity has shown it can in fact heal just as well as medicines.

"Yes, well he's trying to look on the brighter side of life. He's so much more positive now, and I really think it's helping him."

"Exactly. It will. There are a number of documented cases that prove the body will repair itself if, and only if, you are able to channel the energies into healing it. And how do we do that?"

Gina was saying the answer as soon as he finished. "By positive thinking!"

"Excellent! Top pupil."

They made tea and sat back down again. "And parenthood? How is that?"

Gina felt her face glow with pride. The child may not be hers, but she felt so much love towards her. "Better than I'd ever have thought!"

He nodded. "That's good. You know that a child can give you things you may never before have felt possible."

She felt the smile grow across her face. He was so right. She honestly felt for the first time in her life that she had another person she would die for. Considering she'd known Lia only a short time, it scared her how much that love had grown.

Abu and Gina laughed about things for a while. They reminisced on the first few times they'd met, how Gina was so unsure of him. Eventually he'd won her over and had become a good friend. He was able to give her a different outlook on life, and sometimes that was really important to her.

"I'd best be off," she said regretfully. "I have books to sell and coffee to make!"

He nodded. "Look, it doesn't matter if I don't see you so often, my child. You have other responsibilities now. Yeah?"

Gina rolled her eyes. "I can always make time for you, Abu!" They hugged, and then she was on her way.

Chapter Twenty-One

It had been months now. He'd watched her a few times a week. Once again he stood smoking a cigarette and making out he was on a break, but each time he watched and waited. He took a picture or two and followed her, all the time remaining in the shadows. Not once did she ever suspect she was being watched.

What did amuse him was that they were so alike, and yet she didn't know it. The things she had done she'd shrugged off and got on with her life. She snuck around pretending to be this guardian angel, but he knew the real her. He knew who she was and where she'd come from.

He saw her again today. The way she walked with a skip in her step. She was pleased with herself. Invisible blood dripped from her hands leaving a trail that only he could see.

It sickened him.

Thou shalt not kill, and yet here she was, skipping down the pavement without a care in the world. It was almost unbelievable. And yet he was the bogeyman? How many people had he killed?

He'd made an anonymous call that night to the police. He'd mentioned her name. But he'd been naïve. He'd forgotten that she didn't exist. Her name wasn't registered anywhere. Like the lies that fell from her mouth with each breath. Like he was a shadow, she was a phantom.

Innocent people walked past her, unaware of how evil she was. The sweet and angelic girl with the alternative look fooled them. Her voice was quiet and unassuming. She was helpful in her role. But the old lady that smiled at her didn't know the real Gina. The one who was dangerous and a menace to society.

The woman would piss herself scared if she knew that this friendly faced girl roamed the streets at night, beating people up, and trawling for dirty sex. Grabbing men into dark alleys and bending over bins whilst she was pumped hard from behind, not even caring who they were.

He was grinding his teeth in frustration. He knew he was to blame here. He needed her to be around and wanted the challenge, but he'd been slack in his knowledge that she'd eventually find her way back to that house. If he'd anticipated it, then he would've surprised her. Perhaps put up balloons and a *Welcome Home* banner. He liked that idea. His mind worked overtime as his imagination kicked into action. If he'd really known then he could've dug up one of the mounds in the garden, maybe draped the remains throughout the house. He didn't care about Jeff nor his bitch wives. He was cross only because she'd got to

Sweet Vigilante

them first. That was unexpected, truly unexpected in fact. He thought when she escaped, she would disappear completely. Maybe she'd travel and end up in some country that asked few questions and expected nothing from her in return. He could see that.

The truth was he wanted that. He longed for her to disappear so the chase would be so much better. He didn't want to know where she was but wanted to have to hunt her down. He dreamed about feeding on scraps of information and using his own skills to find and follow her trail until eventually he'd surprise her when she least expected it. She'd be settled with her own children, and he'd wander into her life and like a wolf would snatch away her off-spring one by one.

But she'd ruined it. She travelled around thirteen miles into the city and pretty much remained there in the same area ever since. Finding her was simple. All he did was what he did best. Watch and wait.

He saw her and followed her. Then he sent Jeff in to scope her out. It was a test to see whether she'd recognise him. She did.

He was in no hurry. Not now that she had a child. The most wonderful thing in the world in fact. A weakness there for him to see; to exploit, to turn the screw on her emotions and inflict the maximum pain.

He grinned to himself, now calming down. He'd always been impulsive when all he needed to do was to remain chilled and think about how he'd take his own revenge.

He couldn't wait for that.

Chapter Twenty-Two

When Gina got back into work from lunch she was met by a huge grin from Baxter. He stood there with an idiotic look on his face.

"What?" she said. "Have you eaten something funny?"

"Your admirer was back," he said, ignoring her.

"Noah?" she felt her skin flush.

Baxter nodded, then cocked an eyebrow. "Unless you have others?"

"Hardly!"

"I told him you were out at lunch, and with that he simply said he'd pop back later."

Gina felt herself smile. It had been a long time since she'd felt this way about a man. In fact, she struggled to remember if indeed she ever had. Many times, her relationships hadn't lasted after either a sexual encounter or even a single date.

She tried to act casual but inside, her heart was skipping in a way she'd read about but never thought possible. She wanted to ask more questions. She wanted to keep the conversation going. Keep that feeling inside going on and on.

Baxter walked off leaving her to a couple who came in holding hands but soon split apart to look at different sections. She wore a small backpack, and a tight sweatshirt and was big into the generic psychological thrillers. She was quick to pluck the paperbacks from the shelves and read the whole of the blurb. Most appeared to be domestic noirs by female authors. A small smile played on her lips. He, however, was searching very carefully with his eyes over the spines. He was either unsure what he was after or there was something very specific that he was yet to find. It was hard to tell. He favoured tipping the book back so only a small section of the blurb could be seen. He made up his mind quickly. He discounted much and liked little, but eventually he settled on a James Rollins adventure book. He held it loosely in his hand as he walked over to the woman. She had a pile of three books and was still not satisfied. Her eyes roamed the spines, and she juggled the books to help her grab more.

"Found anything?" he asked with a voice that was a lot deeper than Gina had expected. He was being sarcastic.

"I could buy so many," the woman replied – in her element.

They turned to the counter and grinned at Gina. This was a fine example of why she loved her job. The joy that books brought people was great. They were just buying them, and already she could see the excitement of what may lay inside the covers. They

Jim Ody

hadn't even started reading them yet. Whether it was their love of books that had brought them together, or even one of them having introduced the art of reading to the other, it was a mutual joy.

They paid for the books and left satisfied.

Gina thought back to the books she'd read when growing up at the house. There had been a lot of adult books around. It was almost deliberate that these horror and crime books were in the reach of children.

Gina had read some gruesome books but loved them nevertheless. It was escapism for a start, but also a form of education. Even the twisted themes somehow eased the pain she felt inside. It gave her ideas. And strength.

It was what planted the seed to escape.

She was so deep in thought that she didn't see him enter. He walked up slowly, perhaps even a little nervous.

"How was lunch?" Noah said in a voice that hid any sign of nerves.

She looked up, like an elastic cord had pulled her back to reality. "Good," she replied as a stock answer. Then added, "Twice in one day. You are a quick reader!"

He blushed but fought it off. Somewhere under it all was a confident man. "Actually, I wondered whether you wanted to go for coffee some time?" he glanced out to where they sold drinks. "Maybe somewhere else?"

"You don't like the coffee here?" she teased.

"I like it very much, but I'd feel a little self-conscious trying to woo a woman in her own place of work."

Now she blushed. "You looking to woo me?"

He shrugged. "I'm looking to try."

She was nodding before he'd even finished. "Sure."

They arranged to meet later on at *Max it Up*; Gina didn't let on that she knew Max. She couldn't help it. She would always be wary of people and felt so much better when there was somebody around to look out for her.

When Noah had gone, Gina walked with a skip in her step down past the Fantasy section to where Baxter was standing with some New Releases.

"He came back," she said almost with a giggle. She couldn't help the light and happy feeling.

"Prince Charming?"

She nodded. Idly, she picked up a Pratchett novel. She'd never read him and didn't intend to anytime soon. Besides she was just keeping her hands busy. "I've got a date."

"Really?" he said, stopping what he was doing.

"Don't sound so surprised!"

"Gina, I've known you for ages, and I've never known you to ever have a date, or even so much as an interest in a man. Or a woman, for that matter!"

Gina found this amusing. It was true she'd always kept her feelings to herself. When others were talking about their relationships, she'd either remain quiet or move away. She couldn't relate to the whole courtship, dating, or full relationship. Her experiences were very private. Dominating drunken men in the small hours. The words were kept to a minimum. The kisses were without passion and more through a sense of duty. Sometimes they were absent. The whole act was purely for sexual release. It was a side of her that she felt would shock Baxter and the other staff. And that was it. She saw them as staff and not friends. Not that there was an issue. They all tried to be friendly, but she could never give herself over. She knew it was a trust thing. All about her experience. People of her own age got snatched away from her, that's how she saw it.

She hummed to herself as the hands on the clock slowed down. She suddenly felt really lucky. With Lia, Pops, and Lynne, she had a family core. Abu, Baxter and even Max were a slightly wider circle, along with a whole host of important people that were allowed to get only semi-close to her.

And now there was Noah. A biblical name for a wonderful man, she mused.

When she got back to her flat, she threw her arms around Lia. The small child held her tightly back.

"I missed you," Gina said to her, kissing the top of her head.

Lia grinned back. "I missed you, too. But school was great!"

"It was? Why? What did you do?"

"Maths!" the child said this as if it was a real treat. Gina had never been much of a fan of figures. She knew the basics, but her schooling at the house was never that in depth. Most things she learnt from books or later on via the internet, but maths was something that often required explanation or examples. Numbers tended to move around the page when she stared at them hard. She struggled to focus.

Sweet Vigilante

"Mrs Cook gave me twenty questions, and I got most of them right!" She was very pleased with herself.

"That is great, sweetie!"

Pops glanced up from his paper. "She's a real brainbox, I reckon." He looked at Lia and winked, which made her giggle.

Lia talked on about school. She was always excited to go into great detail about her classmates and what they got up to. It was a miracle that she'd been able to put the past behind her and integrate so successfully with the other children.

They all turned as they heard the front door open. Lynne let herself in.

"Hello!" she said, as Lia ran over to her. "Now that's a welcome!"

Lia had really brought something to them all. It was a purpose in life, one they'd not admitted to having before her. Each living out their lives as best they could without admitting as much.

"So," Gina started. That got everyone's attention. "I was just wondering whether you all minded if I popped out to meet someone? Just an hour, or so?"

Pops looked over to Lynne, who smiled back and shrugged. "The lady is quite mysterious," Lynne said.

"Indeed," Pops added. "And who is the lucky person? Do we need to vet them?"

"Have you got a boyfriend?" Lia grinned.

Gina held up her hands. "Look, let's not get carried away. It's just a guy who I met at work. He invited me out for coffee."

Pops waved off what she was saying. "We're joking. Of course you can. Lia is fine with us."

"I know," Gina looked over at Lia. "Are you sure you're okay with this?"

Lia jumped up and down. "Yes, yes, yes!" Gina still felt guilty. The last thing she wanted was for Lia to feel like she was being dropped in favour of someone new.

"Well, if you're sure?"

"Yes!" everyone replied in unison. "Go out and have some fun!"

Chapter Twenty-Three

Gina had tried on the contents of her wardrobe. It was a whole new concept for her and suggested how much this date meant to her.

"You look pretty," Lia said when Gina had finally decided on an outfit.

"Maybe you need glasses," she grinned at the child. Lia giggled at that and curled her forefingers around her thumbs like circles and made her own glasses.

"No, you still look pretty!"

Pops took a step back when he saw her. He almost looked like he might cry.

"You look wonderful. He's a lucky guy. I hope he realises that!"

"You old fool," Gina said, welling up herself before giving them both hugs and heading out the door.

Gina got to the diner right on time – a habit she'd had for a number of years. She walked into the busy establishment and was hit by the smell of fried food. It didn't matter how bad she knew it was for her, she couldn't deny that it smelt so good! She'd tried and tested most things on the menu, too, so she could confirm everything was great.

"Hey, Gina!" Max shouted with a raised hand. She waved back and grinned, Max continued with cooking.

Jim Ody

She saw Noah sitting at a table in the corner. He was deep in thought looking at the menu. She couldn't blame him, there was a lot to choose from.

He had on a fresh black shirt and looked like he'd done all he could to look his best too. That was a good sign, she thought.

When he noticed her, his face lit up. It made Gina feel so wonderful and special. She wasn't sure she'd ever felt like that before.

He stood up like a gentleman and said, "Gina, hi!"

Her heart was beating hard in her chest, but she also felt quite comfortable, albeit a little nervous. She really didn't want to mess things up.

"Hi, Noah," she said and sat down opposite him.

Max appeared just as Noah was about to say something. "Order what you want. It's all on the house, kid," Max said, flashing a glance at them both and clapping his hands together.

"Thanks Max," she said a little nervously, not for any other reason than it felt weird with Max meeting her date.

Her date? She thought. *This was what it was, wasn't it?* She had to stop herself. She'd overthink things and then everything would get weird.

"Anyway, I'll leave you two to it. Have a nice meal. Or coffee, or whatever!" Max was tripping over his own words now. All three of them were caught up in this awkward situation.

"Thanks again!" she called after him as he scooted off. She didn't want him to feel like she was pushing him away. She really did appreciate him.

"You duped me," Noah grinned when Max was far enough away. "You know everyone here, too!"

Gina smiled back. "Not everyone."

She pointed to a teenage waitress with ginger hair and acne. "I don't know her."

It was a good ice-breaker.

"Fiona. She already introduced herself to me."

Gina cocked her head. She felt a pang of jealousy. "Did she now!" They laughed at that. From there, the conversation flowed well. Noah had moved here six months ago, initially due to his work. He had been contracted onto an IT project. However, having done well, the company took him on, and so he moved from Nottingham. It wasn't exactly a million miles away, but he'd clearly realised he liked the place.

Gina remained vague on her past. She didn't believe in lying, so had made up her mind from the beginning that she would answer any questions Noah had, but would not offer details. She was embarrassed about what had happened, but she refused to let it stop her from finding happiness.

"So, you enjoy the bookshop," he asked. "I mean, it's a great place."

"Yeah, it's great. Books are such magical things, and it brings people from all walks of life together."

He nodded, and she went on to tell him about the couple that day. She continued to praise her place of work, explaining how lucky she was and the differences between it and the large chain bookshops.

"So how long have you been a Koontz fan," she asked.

"A long time. I read his books in school. I loved the way you never knew where one of his books would lead you. You could immerse yourself into the story but happily continue knowing it would be fun."

"That's an interesting way of putting it. You do any writing yourself?"

He shrugged and she immediately wondered whether he was being modest. "I expect a lot of readers dabble."

"You any good?"

"If I was then you'd recognise me, right?"

"Fame doesn't always find the gifted," she said. The words appeared from nowhere.

"Now who's flexing their literary muscles."

She was shaking her head at that. "God, no. Authors are self-centred and anti-social. I'm much worse than that!" They both laughed at that.

Of course, time got away from them. Gina wasn't used to that. Chatting on for hours over coffee to someone you have a mutual connection with. She glanced at her watch as subtly as possible. She was having so much fun but knew she had to go home. If nothing else, she was looking forward to sitting with Lia whilst she read.

"Sorry, do you have to go?" Noah said, disappointment evident in his voice.

"Yes, sorry." She was about to mention Lia, but then to explain her would mean to go back through everything. It all seemed a little too much for the first date.

"I've probably been here an hour longer than I intended!"

"I guess I'll take that as a compliment," he said.

Sweet Vigilante

"Most definitely." Silence fell upon them. Gina wanted time to stand still for a little while longer, and Noah wanted to sweep her up into his arms. Both exercised great restraint against what their bodies desired. That was all part of being an adult.

Gina got up and said, "I really enjoyed this. Can we do it again?"

He looked pleased and relieved all at once. Nodding, he said, "That would be great. How about we actually go out for food?"

"Yes, let's do that." She paused, and when she spoke again it was with a cheeky grin. "Perhaps, I'll not have any time constraints, either." He smiled back.

"Tomorrow night?" he added and then looked worried. "Or is that too soon?"

She laughed. "Tomorrow night sounds good."

There was an awkward moment as they got up and walked out. They stopped at the door, both unsure how to end things. In the end they stumbled into each other with a kiss on the cheek. It was a start, and both equally wished for more. There was no rush. They both wanted more, and tomorrow night they could go further if the desire so took them.

Gina said goodbye and headed off home. The familiar journey took her on autopilot as she fantasised about what might have been and at what may happen in the future.

Rain started as she got to her block of flats. She skipped the last couple of steps until she was inside.

Again, she realised just how good she felt.

Lia ran over to her as she walked in through the door. Pops looked up with a smile, and Lynne was still there holding a hand of cards.

Jim Ody

"How was your friend?" Pops asked. His voice teased her slightly, but it was light-hearted. He only wanted the best for her.

"Yes, your fancy-man!" Lynne added.

"I'm too young to have a fancy-man, Lynne!"

Lynne giggled and fanned herself with the cards. "You're not too young, and I'm not too old!"

"I don't know about that!" Pops added.

"I've won nearly every time!" Lia said with excitement.

"I'm never playing for money," Pops said deadpan, shaking his head in mock defeat.

"So," Lynne said. "You deflected the question. How was he?"

Gina felt herself glow, but in a smaller voice than normal uttered, "A real gentleman."

"That's the guy you want," Pops said nodding approval. "Just like me."

"You old fool," Lynne said, and then turned to Gina. "I'm pleased for you, dear."

"He wants us to go out for a meal tomorrow night," Gina said. "Maybe more." She instantly regretted saying the last bit and wasn't sure why she did.

"Really? So go then!" Lynne replied before Gina could finish. Then she leaned in and whispered, "Us women have needs, too."

"You think it's a good idea?"

"You want him running off with some other girl? No, strike whilst his iron's hard."

"Hot," Pops laughed. "The phrase is strike while the iron's hot."

Lynne laughed, "Freudian slip, I'm afraid." She glanced at Pops, who for the first time ever looked a little embarrassed.

"Yes, well," he stammered.

There was a sudden round of giggling.

"She's actually right for once," Pops agreed. "It doesn't happen very often. We'll look after Lia, won't we, kid?"

Lia shrugged. "I guess."

"Well, I know," Pops said in a way that brought a smile from her. "You know what else this old fool knows?"

Lia was all wide-eyed now. "No, what?"

"Ice-cream is on special down the road, so I reckon if we get a tub tomorrow, then we could sit in and watch some cartoons and eat ice-cream, yeah?"

"Yeah!"

It was a wonderful sight to watch. Lia had fit in so well, and it had definitely brought Pops and Lynne closer together. Before, they had bickered like old friends, but now there was something there. It was almost like they were playing at being grandparents. Possibly making irons hard, too, but Gina didn't need to know that.

Lynne got up. She groaned a little as she moved.

"You okay, old woman?" Pops teased.

"Yeah," she said. "I think since cutting back on the booze I'm feeling my age." She rubbed her hip.

"So you were drunk all the time to numb the pain of coming round!"

"I thought so," she continued. "But it turns out it's not bad around here sober either!"

Jim Ody

"You want me to walk you out?" Pops added getting up. This was a move Gina had not seen before.

"Don't be silly. You're as old as God. I don't want to put you to any trouble."

"It's no bother."

She looked at him seriously, and said, "Okay then. Oh, and there's something I need you to take a look at around mine."

"Ah-ha," he said, suddenly with a spring in his step.

Gina held up a hand. "See you tomorrow."

Lynne turned to her. "Get some sleep, Gina. You want to look your best for your date tomorrow, right?"

"I guess so."

Ten minutes later and Lia was sitting on the bed listening to Gina read a story about a boy. One who always seemed to get into trouble.

Pops came back an hour later. He didn't mention what he needed to check out, but he smelt strongly of Lynne's perfume. Gina smiled to herself. She was pleased for them both.

Chapter Twenty-Four

He had watched her that evening. He stayed in the shadows and glanced periodically through the window of the diner. He saw the way they laughed and joked. They were getting to know each other.

It made him sick. She had a child to look after, and yet here she was touting for clients in what amounted to a fancier version of a greasy-spoon.

He couldn't understand how she could just carry on like nothing was wrong. She was a murderer. And here she was snuggling up with some guy she'd only just met. She'd neglected the little brat to go and meet this bloke. She'd not give her a second thought as she dropped her knickers and spread her legs for her new man. That would come later on of course, but it would still happen.

He smoked a cigarette to calm his nerves. In fact, he smoked a handful, one after another, hoping the nicotine would mellow his mood.

It didn't.

Jim Ody

He crossed the road and sat down in the doorway of a shop. He looked like a homeless man. There were enough of those lost fuckers around, so he blended in just fine.

An hour or so later he watched them leave. He was surprised when they went their separate ways. Maybe she was charging too much. Perhaps he was going home to his wife and kids. Who fucking knew?

He wondered which one he would follow.

He knew where she lived so he got up, flicked the cigarette into the gutter, and followed Romeo.

The guy was medium height and looked like he was into fitness. Some fucking gym-rat, no doubt. Pumping a few weights and then taking pictures of himself in the mirror. He knew the sort. Probably loved his Instagram account and pretended to be annoyed at the female attention he got.

He hated the fact that this guy was walking quickly. These were annoyingly happy steps.

He crossed over the road and shot down an alleyway, before grabbing in his pocket for his keys.

The guy slowed down and stayed back, noting the small house squashed within a terrace. It was a new estate, only four or five years old. A large dairy used to occupy the area, providing employment for hundreds of people. Like a lot of industry, it closed down, became a vacant shell for youngsters to mess around in before it was sold, flattened, and a contemporary village was planted. It had sprung up in a matter of months like magic beans.

He watched the front door close. He was well into double figures of things he hated about the man.

He wasn't good enough for Gina. His Gina. The guy didn't know her the way he did.

Filled with rage, he set about letting off some steam.

Chapter Twenty-Five

Gina was now getting used to waking up gently and no longer covered in sweat. She began to dream like a normal person, first mundane situations and then the odd tantalising scene with a mystery man, one she couldn't see his face but she was strongly attracted to. Her date had clearly filled her mind with more erotic thoughts in the empty rooms she'd cleared out that used to harbour so much pain.

Her one worry surrounded her night time activities. She had only gone out a couple of nights in the past month. Tiredness had no problem in finding her, and without the insomnia or nightmares, she was sleeping through and feeling so much better for it the next day.

Lia was chatty as she sat down for breakfast. Gina placed a glass of milk in front of her, as the little girl mumbled through a toast-filled mouth something about unicorns.

"What was?" Gina said with a smile. "Try swallowing your food before you tell me. I don't want you choking!"

Pops nodded. "You'll end up in hospital like me!"

Lia laughed and chewed faster.

It was at that point Gina saw over her shoulder the local news.

A heavily made-up anchor stood looking incredibly serious. They were professional and concerned:

"The girl was attacked in the small hours. This is the third one in the past week, although the police cannot confirm whether the incidents are connected…"

Gina threw a glance over at Pops who looked back at her with a knowing look. Their faces seemed void of expression but their eyes couldn't hold back what they felt inside.

Gina felt guilty. Her stomach hit the floor.

She knew it was stupid. She was not a superhero. She could not be expected to walk the streets and scare off criminals. This wasn't a comic book but real life. Crime flourishes everywhere. An oil stain on society's best jacket. An inevitability that can never be eradicated by just one person and a stretched police force.

Sweet Vigilante

"So, as I was saying," Lia said with enthusiasm and a now empty mouth. "The unicorn was huge, and pink! When it breathed, glitter shot out!"

"Glitter?" Gina replied, distracted. She looked over again at Pops who winked at her. It was a gesture, less of fun but one of reassurance. He knew. He could see inside her.

Not for the first time, she wondered whether she really was doing the right thing in taking on Lia. *Did the girl deserve a more traditional family?* But it was the thought that her actions could have had anything to do with the sudden spate of crime that really worried her. The mash-up of parenting and random vigilante acts was not something that *mumsnet* would approve. A mother was meant to offer a safe environment for a child and not slip out into the night and trawl the streets for society's lowlifes. And of course, she didn't use to just fight crime, sometimes she willingly went off with unscrupulous individuals just to numb the pain of her past.

"Have a good day. Remember how good things are," Pops said as she left to take Lia to school. "You have your own life to live." He held her gaze for a couple of beats, and it was more in what he didn't say that said the most. He was telling her it wasn't her fault.

"I know," she replied.

"And your date tonight!" he added. Lia giggled.

"I know!" she said again as Lia made kissy-sounds.

Gina was excited inside. This was something she wasn't use to. An unexpected ride lay ahead, and every time her thoughts lingered on him, her tummy jiggled inside. *Was this love?* She wondered but dismissed the notion just as quickly. Surely it was too soon to be thinking along those lines? And then the realisation of the whole situation hit her hard. Her rational side kicking in and told her it was her experience that was making this a bigger deal than it needed to be. She shouldn't get her hopes up on a handsome book geek. She wondered whether he shared the same nerves as she had, or was this a normal scenario he regularly played out? She remembered how nervous he looked the night before and the effort he'd put in to look good, too, and that made her feel a little better.

She kissed Lia on the forehead. She soon merged into a group of girls. They welcomed her, grinned at each other and went off disappearing into school.

Gina watched her like any other proud parent. Her heart ached at the sudden loss. She worried all the time when she wasn't with her.

The morning flew by. Gina had always enjoyed work. Baxter seemed just as excited about her date as she was and kept asking her more and more questions. She was happy to comply.

"You going to do the dirty with him tonight?" Baxter said in a playful way. From another guy it might've seemed intrusive, or vulgar, but Baxter was Baxter. He had this way of putting a person at ease, often getting them to say a lot more than they were expecting to say.

Gina never drank alcohol around Baxter. Loose lips sink ships and all of that jazz.

"I dunno," she admitted. Of course, Baxter was unaware of her nocturnal prowling and so assumed her to be almost virginal.

Sweet Vigilante

"Hmmm, interesting. Not denying the possibilities, either!"

She picked up a pile of new books, and as she walked past him slowed and whispered, "Not with that arse!" and walked off. Baxter was left silenced and with his jaw on the floor.

The afternoon predictably dragged. Even in the job she loved, her mind was filled with Noah. She pictured his smile and was then embarrassed at her dreamy state. She worried slightly at what might happen after. The physical aspect made her nervous as she'd never been tender with a man. Just quick and feverish. It all happened with few words and little contact that was anything but sweet and gentle. Would he be shocked at her wild side? Could she be anything but that? She tried to snap out of it as she knew she was overthinking everything again. It was only their second date!

The meeting the day before had been great, but they'd barely scratched the surface. There was still so much to learn, and of course so much for her to tell him. She hoped he'd understand.

Later at the flat she fussed over things to wear, most of which she'd tried on the night before. She read too much into every item of clothing, convinced each said something different about her. She didn't want to go with her usual tight vest and leather jacket for fear of scaring him away. Noah was used to seeing her toned down for work. He didn't know about the tattoos she had hidden about her body. They were all very personal to her. None were a fashion statement or an act of rebellion. They were more deliberate scars that border on being self-harm; they provided her with the

Jim Ody

pain, and pictorial memory she felt she needed to get over her past.

At first, she tried on a flimsy dress, but the spaghetti straps gave glimpses of her ink, and she knew this would only cascade into a conversation best left out of a second date. Her bed soon piled up with discarded clothes as she whittled her choices down to the final two. A shirt, or a flowing long-sleeved top.

She stood at her full-length mirror, each top still on a hanger and held in front of her. She moved left and right imagining herself wearing each.

She caught a glimpse of the little face grinning at her.

"You'll look pretty in either, Mummy," the voice said very matter-of-factly.

In an instant, Gina felt her eyes water. It was such a beautifully innocent thing to say. Gina loved being referred to as Mummy. She turned around, crouched down, and beckoned the girl towards her outstretched arms.

"Thank you, honey."

They embraced long and hard. "Maybe the white one," Lia said.

"You think?"

She nodded. "You'll look so pretty. Like last night. I bet he liked what you wore then, too?"

She nodded. "I think so."

The white one it was. A long-sleeved, floaty baggy arms top, over her jeans.

"Don't you look great," Pops said after she'd dressed and spent twenty minutes applying make-up.

"You're too kind."

Sweet Vigilante

She gave out kisses and hugs, took a deep breath, and was on her way.

Chapter Twenty-Six

Time moved slowly when you watched it, and for Gina this was certainly the case. It did nothing for her nerves either. Her stomach felt so swimmy that she wasn't sure how she'd be able to eat anything.

The waiter walked over and filled up her wine glass, flashing a consolation smile. He tried not to judge and remain professional and impartial. But under the professionalism he was wondering the same thing as she was.

Gina smiled back, but it was one of those that you feel the movement of each muscle, such was the effort.

Ten minutes late was not ideal. But the hands on the clock had since moved on and she was now about to finish her second glass of red wine. The first one had been for courage, the second was something to do. The waiting only made her hands need to do something, and they automatically held the glass and lifted it to her lips.

Sweet Vigilante

Her glances towards the door became mechanical, broken only by looks at her wristwatch and the screen of her phone. Each one followed the other, her disappointment growing with each cycle.

At first, she'd made up excuses for him. Woven a handful of tales that would keep a man from a woman. She even smiled, thinking how this might be an amusing story to whisper into the dead of night as they lay naked together.

Or perhaps on their wedding day.

Gina had a lot of patience. It had been the way of her upbringing. Things happened on other people's terms. She had a life of waiting. This was nothing new. Nothing good came from rushing things.

It would be worth it.

A couple in the corner had clocked her and were whispering and throwing over glances. They shared a joke at her expense. A woman walking back from the toilet caught her eye and then just as quickly looked away. Perhaps she didn't want the bad luck to be transferred to her. Everyone else was too absorbed in either their food or company to have noticed her.

By thirty-five minutes she had sent him a message. Light-hearted and joking. By forty-five minutes, she began to feel deflated. And then rejected and alone.

The waiter was already walking towards her as she caught his eye.

"The bill please," she said, her voice almost letting her down.

"No bill. No charge, madam," he said. "He or she has missed a wonderful opportunity, if I may say so."

Jim Ody

She glanced over him. A young Turkish guy, polite, and either wonderful at customer service, or a real charmer. She couldn't quite decide. It didn't matter.

"Thank you," was all she could come up with. She got up, and feeling slightly tipsy from two large glasses of wine on an empty stomach, walked out of the restaurant. She felt the pity stares all around her. Heads bowed in whispers, the men wondered why, and the women were glad not to be her.

She refused to go straight home. Instead, she let the night swallow her up. Each side of the street had bars spilling light and laughter out with a promise of a good time.

The Queen's Tap pub stood next door, and the sound of music and fun drew her in like an addict. A couple stood outside doing their best to abuse their lungs with watered-down tobacco. Through the clouds of vapour they barely saw her. They barely even saw each other. To them she was just another generic woman meeting friends.

The chatter erupted as she pushed open the door. Some edgy pop song played out, its pulsating bass line sending invisible shockwaves past her. She pushed her way through the crowds towards the bar. Men stared at her with lustful eyes, but she did her very best to ignore them. She was the one playing the silent tune to which they would dance. She hated men again.

It was standard practise that an attractive woman would get served more quickly than a man. It was not a point feminists would either acknowledge or complain about, but it happened. It was accepted by most people – men included – to be a normal practise, and so it was

Sweet Vigilante

of no surprise that the female bartender turned to her, smiled, and said, "What can I get you?"

Gina grabbed her glass of whisky. The golden liquid chased its tail around the bottom of the glass with her movement, and the ice cubes did their best to dilute the fun as they clattered against the glass.

She hid herself away in the corner. Maybe it was an act of self-pity, or perhaps she was setting her own honeytrap. She wasn't thinking straight. She was on autopilot playing a role of her subconscious. No rules; just going with her body. This was nature at its best.

The truth was she was hurt. It was a horrible feeling. She could take the physical pain. She'd been dealt enough of that. To a point it served a purpose. It controlled her and showed her who was boss. From the times back at the house when she'd dared to speak out, she soon knew what it felt like to be hit by a man. Not just to be silenced, but to be taught a lesson.

The shock and explosion of pain from the nerves in the face was easy to remember, but soon anger became an anaesthetic. And her planned escape made it tolerable.

But this was different. It came from within her; the pit of her stomach, and ached deep within her heart. She felt disappointed and let down. Not only didn't he show, but he didn't even bother with a lame excuse. Nothing. Radio silence from a hole that still grew in her heart.

She glanced across the pub. Groups of people her age drank and at least pretended to be having the time of their lives. She couldn't find another single person who looked as sad as she did. For that, on some level, she was thankful.

Jim Ody

She took a swig of the liquid fire and for a second closed her eyes. She thought back to the first week she'd been on the streets. After the first guy had approached her.

Debased her.

That was a new level of shame for her.

But shame presents itself to you when you acknowledge you are letting down the people in your life. At that point, she was only letting herself down, but the justification was survival. It was easier to accept.

She had spent a cold and sleepless night huddled under a damp railway bridge. This was followed by a day sat in old doorways as the guilt of passers-by washed over her. She had expected the shame of pity, but that wasn't what she got. Either they refused to acknowledge her or looked down at her like she was to blame. She was judged immediately and then forgotten in a heartbeat. So was nothing. Less than nothing, in fact.

The next night she was propositioned again. With few words, and a lack of enthusiasm, desperation took hold of her and this time, was rewarded. Whilst wiping herself clean, she was given cash. Crumpled notes thrust into her shaking hand. She remembered looking at it and wondering whether it was worth it. For both him and her. She had grabbed a meal at the diner. And met Max for the first time.

He looked her over and knew the usual grease-based meal wasn't exactly what she needed. He instead made her a soup and a warm drink as the patrons came and went. At no point did he ask her to leave. He also never asked her any questions. He just allowed her to huddle in the corner, warm up, and fill her stomach.

"Come back tomorrow, I'll make you something else," he said, hoping she'd return.

She did.

Gina spent a week on the streets, making money and forgetting who she was, before one night at the diner an old guy walked in. Max nodded over to her, and the old guy sat down in front of her.

"You want something from me?" she asked, slightly aggressively. That was how it was on the streets. Always expect the worst and you'll never be disappointed.

"Not what you think," he said. He had kind eyes. He looked like he'd felt loss. She wondered what weird shit he was into.

"Then what do you want?"

The old guy was of course Pops. He looked all around as if surveying the place.

"You like it here?" he asked.

She shrugged. "Sure. It's warm and dry, and Max gives me free food."

Pops nodded. "And where do you go from here?"

"Sleep. I go to sleep."

"You sleep on the streets? Or have you got a place?"

She took a deep breath. She looked all around, her eyes darting, and her mind racing.

"I'd best be off," she said, and made to move.

"Hold on, now. Look, I'm a lonely old man. I live on my own. I'm only looking to help you. Nothing more."

Jim Ody

"Right," she said in a disbelieving tone. "You're old enough to be my grandpa, and you want a young girl moving in with you? I see how this is. You're hardly Richard Gere, and I'm not Julia Roberts."

"She makes old movie references to me! I'm older than Richard Gere!"

"And? What d'you want?" She spoke with a hard edge to her voice. Kindness only got street urchins killed.

Pops was waving this off. He even laughed. "I'm not looking for any of that nonsense, girl. I've women my own age I can call on if I want a bit of slap and tickle. No, I'm just saying, I have a place with a spare room if you want it."

"Okay," she was still unconvinced.

"Stay a few days. You want to leave, then leave. I'm not looking to force you to do anything."

"I can leave when I want?"

He nodded. "Tell whoever you want, if it makes you feel better."

"You're not going to molest me?"

"Hey Max?" he shouted.

Max looked up. "Yeah?"

"Am I going to molest her?"

Max laughed, all deep and throaty. "You couldn't if you wanted to, you old fool!"

Gina gave half a smile. She was warming to these two. "I'm not sure whether or not I should feel good about that answer."

"Hey kid?" Max shouted, waddling over. "He's a good man. I'd trust him with my life."

She shrugged, and nodded. "Fine," she said.

Sweet Vigilante

From that night on. She was never molested and so never left.

"You want company?" A handsome guy said bringing Gina back to reality. He was well-dressed, carrying a pint, and behind him a group of equally dapper men nudged and smiled over.

She looked up at him. "I was just leaving," she said and got up. He was lost for words, clearly not used to the knock back.

She glanced over at his friends as she walked by. They were about to explode with laughter at their mate. This was what constituted entertainment to them, she guessed. Sad little boys who once rolled around in the mud together grew up to frequent pubs and roll around drunk on the floor together.

The night was dark. The cool air teased around her as she walked away. She followed the street towards the alleyway and walked down it. It was the wrong direction to her flat, but sometimes she felt like she owned the night.

The familiar bridge under the railway came into view. She spotted the area where – scared – she'd spent that first night alone. The smell of urine was thick in the air. She could almost cry at the memories. They were so vivid.

She took a deep breath, and checked her phone once again.

Still nothing.

She turned and made her way back.

And then she heard the scream.

She ran towards the building, turned the corner and saw a guy pushing a woman to the ground.

"Hey!" she shouted as she got closer.

Jim Ody

The face was a mask of evil. All pointy and unhealthy.

"Stay away, bitch!" he shouted, showing her his fist.

Gina hated bullies. This was more than that. It was just about taking control. He was after something else.

"Leave her alone, and get lost," she said calmly.

"Or what?" he coaxed.

"You don't want to know."

He laughed and jumped forward at her, looking to tackle her to the ground and bending over to grab her waist.

Gina brought up her knee, looking to connect with his chin. The guy managed to turn his head at the last second but still caught it full on his cheekbone.

She collapsed on top of him and pulled one of his arms back behind him.

"Okay! Okay!" he pleaded.

Gina motioned to the girl. "Are you hurt?"

The girl shook her head.

"Go on. Stay away from these alleys. Trash like this wanders around preying on women because he can't get one of his own!" Her words were hissed through her teeth. The anger inside was enough to tip her over the edge, and she had to work hard to pull back. She knew from experience that she could kill again.

He went to say something, but she applied just enough pressure for him to decide against it.

"Thank you," the girl said, grabbing her bag and running off.

Gina reached into her bag and pulled out some cable ties.

"Woah!" he said and wriggled like the snake he was. She smiled at him, and with an open hand smashed her palm into his nose.

As his hands shot to his face, she slipped the cable ties on, flipping him to pull them behind his back. Instead of trying to wrestle them onto his ankles, too, she did the next best thing, undid his trousers and pulled them down. With his hands behind his back he couldn't pull them up or take them off.

"Have a good night," she said, putting her mobile away.

She'd sent a text to her friend on the police force. They'd pick the guy up soon. They'd have nothing to hold him on, but he'd spend the night locked up anyway. Maybe he'd think about his actions next time, she thought.

Satisfied the night hadn't been a total failure, Gina headed back to the flat. Alone.

Tomorrow she'd have to answer questions, but tomorrow was another day.

Jim Ody

Sweet Vigilante

Chapter Twenty-Seven

The thing about gravity is that something hanging rarely remains still. A breeze is enough to move an object even of substancial weight. The thing wants to be on the ground and longs to be there.

The erroneous object was displayed like some sort of macabre art-work. Twitching in the moonlight waiting to be found. It was pale and well past its best. The body-shaped pendulum swung ever so slightly from the street light in a deserted part of the city. Specifically chosen for its location, the victim had not been random. He had been targeted, followed, attacked and displayed, all because of a jealous hatred.

An urban fox cracked the night with its cry. Eerie, lonely, and abandoned, the lifeless soul would remain there until it was found. There was no doubt that this was not a suicide. It wasn't even made to look like one. The drying clots of blood had raced down the body from the gaping smile in the throat, only to slow to a sticky membrane as the blood got too thin to run anymore. In some cases, it was nothing but a dried smear. A well-executed plan had played out exactly as the perpetrator had intended. And yet, there was still a whole hungry hole where he assumed satisfaction would be fulfilled.

A late-night reveller, taking a wrong turn and in an inebriated state, would eventually find the man. It would take some time before a call was made to the emergency services, and even longer for the man to be able to direct the police to the location. The man asked for his own mother a couple of times but the twenty-five-year-old dispatcher was unable to help him there.

Hours later, an investigator would conclude that a vicious attack had taken place with seemingly no clear motive. It was nothing but an evil and unwarranted act.

The man's wallet – fat with cash – was untouched in his jeans pocket. His mobile and keys were awkwardly embraced in his other front pocket, completely untouched.

In the days to come the man would be identified. The case was rapidly cooling down before it had even got into full swing.

His name was Noah Thomas, and he was last seen going out on a date. He was picked up on a CCTV camera not far from where he lived in a new part of the city.

His date was seen on the other side of town in the timeframe it was thought the murder took place. It was clear that she was waiting for him, and phone records also backed that up. There were an incredible amount of worried text messages from her.

Jim Ody

The other strange thing about the case was that his shirt had been ripped open, and a large star had been carved on his chest.

But not only that, below – and written in his blood – were some words.

Chapter Twenty-Eight

Pops tried to pretend that he was reading. Of course, he wasn't. He was waiting up for her. He was desperate to hear how her date had gone. The longer she was gone, the more he assumed it had gone well.

He'd begun the night by watching a rerun of *Jonathan Creek*. He'd seen it before, and even knowing the outcome he still enjoyed watching it again. Then he turned the television off and picked up the paperback.

He knew he shouldn't stay up. But she was the daughter he'd never had. On some level he regretted that, so this was his chance. Lia was tucked up in bed, and he had nothing to do but think about Gina. He was so proud of how she had turned her life around. Most people would've been traumatised by what she'd been through. That would be normal, but she showed guts and determination not to let things get her down. Not only that, she had this ingrained need to help others.

He was so proud.

Jim Ody

Some nights he used to wake up to the sound of her leaving the flat. He knew where she was going and what she was doing. How could he not? Somehow, despite a lack of connection in their genes, they had followed the same path. They were both good people who loved to help. He liked to think of them as an emergency service. It was silly, he knew. But there you go.

The issue was it was never enough. He could never feel good about what they'd done, as there was always so much more to do. A lot of people were inherently evil or harboured dark thoughts that, after alcohol, or the draw of the night, changed their perception of right and wrong.

Look closely, and most perpetrators were victims at some point or had felt forced into their behaviours. But then the spirals were never ending, and it could be easy to make the deterioration of mankind a blameless act. That wasn't right; people had to be held accountable. And other people were just born evil.

She walked in through the door, but her face didn't look like she'd had a great night. He picked up on it immediately.

"Okay?" he asked.

"He didn't show," she said, and at that point her hard shell melted. He scooped her up in arms that had begun to get frailer, and she sobbed into his white shirt.

"His loss," he said to her as he smoothed her hair. He felt sad and angry all at once. He'd never had children, and this scene near on broke his heart.

"He didn't even call, or answer me," she said sniffing, struggling to keep a lid on her feelings. Sometimes once you spoke your emotions out loud the sound opened up the floodgates.

"You're late back," he said, and looked at her knuckles. They were red and slightly puffy.

"I waited almost an hour, then I went for a drink."

"And?" he pressed with a sly grin.

"I beat a guy up," she laughed through the tears.

"Good girl!"

He showed her to her seat like she'd never been there before.

"Cocoa?" he asked and knew she wouldn't say no.

"That would be great." She might've been out fighting, but she still loved to have the old man look after her when she got home.

They sat there for an hour until the clock moved towards the smaller numbers, talking about their times together. It was all about knowing what you had, and Pops did his best to let her know that they all loved her. If nothing else, she had an old fool and a beautiful little girl, even if most other men were arseholes!

Gina stood up. "Pops? I saw your scrapbook."

"I know," he replied.

"I'm sorry, I shouldn't've been nosing around."

He didn't look worried at all. "I thought you probably would."

"You're a hero. You helped people."

"We both help people," he said.

She nodded. "I love you, Pops."

"I love you, too." Gina raised a hand and left for her room. It was a conversation they would properly have sometime. Just not tonight.

She went to the sleeping princess, already feeling a lot better. She could watch her sleep all night, and despite everything, Gina kissed her forehead, slipped into bed, and fell into a deep sleep.

Of course, she was completely unaware that the body of her date had now been found, and she would have questions to answer the next day.

Throughout the night Gina tossed and turned. Her mind fed her brain confusing movie clips. Jumbled up scenes bouncing back and forth from the house to the flat. Often, the details were conflicting. They were out of context and continuity the way that dreams were, but in the morning, she felt almost as tired as when she had gone to bed.

"You were making noises," Lia said sweetly.

Gina smiled at the little girl, she felt energised just by looking at her.

"I'm sorry, Sweetie. Did I wake you?"

The girl shook her head in the over-exaggerated way kids do. "Of course not, silly! It was when I got up for a wee."

"Come here!" Gina said, pulling her in tightly.

Gina showered and grabbed a coffee, whilst Lia got ready for school.

The news was on in the background, but they were all laughing too much to hear. There was a reporter standing with a microphone and looking serious. Behind her there was a glimpse of blue and white police tape.

"So, I get to stand up and read to the class," Lia was saying, even as a picture of Noah flashed onto the screen. Gina was fully engaged, picturing this sweet

Sweet Vigilante

little girl standing up proudly, talking about kittens and how they make great pets. She was unaware of what was going on in the local news. Things moved quickly to politics, and then it was on to the weather.

The morning rush was already on, and before they all knew it, they were all off on their separate ways.

Baxter was there waiting for Gina as she got to work. He was looking at her with mischief in his eyes, expecting a lot of blushing whilst he teased her like a little sister. But he soon understood that things hadn't gone as planned.

"What happened?" he said. His smile had disappeared, replaced by concern.

"He didn't show," she said, taking off her jacket and putting it out the back.

"What? But he was into you. I could tell."

"Clearly not enough," she shrugged, turning back on herself and walking out towards the counter.

Baxter stood there, suddenly unsure what to do. He was a joker, but in these sensitive moments he felt awkward and unsure how to handle the situation.

"I'm sure there's a perfectly good explanation," he offered.

"Maybe." Gina was done with guessing. She wouldn't chase him anymore. In fact, she liked that she was done with men.

For the rest of the morning, Gina busied herself as best she could. There were always things that needed to be done, and a steady trickle of people was enough to keep her occupied.

At lunch, she slipped off to see Abu. She was feeling down and needed his spiritual insight.

Jim Ody

"Come in," she heard him say as she opened the door. He walked forward with a mug and handed it to her.

"How did you know?" she said, doing her best to break into a smile. She was sceptical to a point, but Abu had an aura about him that made him mystical. He was so in touch with the powers of the world – perhaps even other worlds. Forces that could barely be recognised, he was able to channel.

"For a start," he smiled. "It's been a few days. I also understand from sources that you have been dating." He winked. It seemed completely out of character for him.

She blushed. "I was," she started. "It was brief, and now it's over."

"You believe that?"

She blew into the mug and then took a sip. "I know that. He stood me up and ignored all of my messages. What sort of a man does that?"

"Perhaps he had his reasons."

"They had better be good!"

They sat down on the floor cross-legged. The silence fell around them, but was never uncomfortable. Abu had always insisted on the importance of reflection. He often lectured on how the world moved too fast to enjoy the things that people had achieved. People were too quick to move on to something else, always looking for something better and never appreciating what they had created. Nor did they look over what they'd achieved, no matter how small. Each and every experience moulds a person, and yet it's easily forgotten.

Sweet Vigilante

"It's good that you're dating," he said softly. His voice had a calmness to it.

"I'm hardly dating. I went on one date. I have no more planned."

Abu glanced over. His look spoke of her missing the point. "The fact you went on one suggests you've decided to take the next step."

She went to protest, but he held up his hand. "Whatever *you* think!"

Defeated, she nodded. It was true. She knew deep down that she was accepting she could be normal and perhaps have a partner. Maybe even get married one day.

"I just wanted to be normal."

"You are normal, Gina. I actually don't think you do want to be like others."

"You know what I mean."

"Put down your mug, let's chant," he said, and she followed suit. For the next ten minutes they chanted and then meditated. She didn't always believe in the powers, but there was no doubting that when she committed to it, it was good. It was easy to dismiss what we didn't understand, but she knew from her own experiences that life wasn't always black and white. Each person was different, and that was okay.

Gina said goodbye to Abu and left his place feeling a whole lot better.

That was until she got into work and saw two police officers waiting to speak to her.

"Hi, Gina," the taller of the two males said to her. He was officious, in his twenties, and looked like he could chase down most criminals. "We'd like to talk to you about Noah Thomas."

"Noah?" she said. "Um, the only Noah… I mean. I didn't know his surname."

The other officer was scouting out the place. "Have you got somewhere quiet where we can speak?" he said. They were conscious not to make a scene. Police in a commercial establishment were generally bad for business.

Baxter had been hovering around and said, "Go and use the staff room." He looked worried, both for Gina and a little for his business.

Gina had no idea what it was about.

Chapter Twenty-Nine

When they broke the news to her, she couldn't believe it.

"Dead?" she grabbed the chair and almost collapsed into it. She couldn't believe how hard it hit her. A guy she'd only known for a number of days.

But she'd felt it. They'd had a connection, and maybe it was just the excitement of infatuation, but what if it wasn't? What if that was her only chance to find her soulmate? All of those thoughts ran through her mind.

They both nodded. "How did you know him?"

Gina shook her head. Her eyes were blank and lifeless. She took a deep breath, "He came in here a few days ago," the words dried up. She looked past them.

"Had you ever seen him before?"

"No, never. He came in again the same day and asked me out for coffee."

"You went?" the officer pressed. "For coffee?"

She nodded, glancing briefly at him to acknowledge. "Yes, it was great." A small smile flashed on her lips. "I really thought we might have something. He seemed nice. We arranged to go out for a meal."

"On a date?"

She nodded aware she was blushing. "Yes." Her head dropped down. "But he never showed up. I waited an hour for him."

"Wow," the shorter guy said. "That is a long time."

Gina nibbled her bottom lip. "I… I've never been on a date before. I didn't want to give up on him." She felt her face flush with embarrassment once again. She'd said too much. She was finding this really hard.

"What did you know about him?" The officer asked, and then quickly added, "I know you'd just met."

She puffed out her cheeks, and let the question float around for a while. "Not a lot. I mean, I knew where he worked and where he lived. I knew he loved Jack Nicholson movies and classic rock. He told me about a gig at Wembley he'd been to where he'd seen Bon Jovi. He had got within ten feet of the front. He spoke like it was one of his happiest memories."

They nodded again, letting her speak. Of course, everyone within earshot knew that Noah's feeling towards his experiences at a stadium gig twenty years ago was hardly going to give them any revelations, but they also knew that important details appeared in the unlikeliest of places.

Baxter knocked on the door at one stage, apologised, and handed over a coffee to Gina.

Sweet Vigilante

"I thought you might like this," he said with a sympathetic smile. He didn't wait for a response, placed it on the table in front of her, nodded at the police officers, and left the room.

The officers looked longingly at the coffee. Their faces suggested they would've liked a cup, too, but they remained professional. They talked some more, asking general questions about where she went after the restaurant. There were enough people who would be able to corroborate her story, should it come to that. Gina wasn't worried. She felt a whole host of emotions but worry wasn't one of them.

Gina could tell the questions were coming to an end. Both officers looked satisfied with her responses.

And then her mobile went.

It was Pops. He never called her unless it was an emergency. She didn't hesitate to answer it.

"Is everything alright?" she asked, instantly in a panic.

"She's gone," he said to her, an unusual shake in his voice.

"What?" she stood up quickly, the chair fell over. The police looked alarmed. "What? How?"

"A teacher said that her father had come for her. Gina! They just let her go off with him."

"Okay, I'll be right there. I have the police with me."

He seemed even more worried and panicked. "Why? What's going on there? Are you okay?"

"I'm fine," she said. "Stay at the school."

"I will."

She clicked the phone and looked at the police officers.

"Someone has taken my daughter out of school. We don't know where she is."

"Hold on," the taller one said, placing a hand on her arm. "Maybe someone else picked her up? A relative? Or a friend?"

Gina shook her head vehemently. "No. The only three people that have ever picked her up are me, Pops, and his female friend from in the next flat."

"Okay," he said and looked at his colleague. "Call it in, and we'll take her over there."

"Thank you," she said. "I can't lose her. She's everything to me."

They nodded, but inside they knew that something wasn't right. This was England, a normal person didn't have one person close to them murdered one day and another person abducted the next. This wasn't the movies. There was something else going on here. Even though this lady seemed innocent, she appeared to have somebody obsessed with her. That meant trouble.

On another day, Gina might've felt self-conscious getting into the back of a police car, but all she could think about was Lia. She sat back, her hands running through her mind along with pictures of her sweet little girl.

The drive to the school was only a few minutes but everything seemed to slow the journey; traffic lights, and heavy traffic pouring out onto the roads, and Gina's mind was racing with a thousand thoughts. Not one of them positive.

When the police car pulled to a stop, she grabbed the door latch, but of course the child locks were on, it just made a noise without opening. A low guttural sound came from her in frustration. The policeman in front quickly got out and opened the door for her. Any onlookers would see the strange sight of a woman bursting out of the police car.

Tears streamed down Gina's cheeks as she was confronted by two ladies from the school. One looked officious and very serious, and the other had her head hung low and looked like she'd been crying. Pops was standing there, too, and he scooped her up in his arms.

"What happened?" Gina said, firstly to Pops and then to the women behind.

The stern lady was quick with a response. "A gentleman claiming to be Lia's father turned up and said he had been sent to pick her up today as you were stuck in traffic."

"What?" Gina looked at Pops.

"I'm sorry, love. I was late. I got caught on a phone call. I couldn't get off." He looked devastated. She could never blame him.

She nodded to him, and held him tight. "But I thought she was only allowed to leave with the three designated people? We filled in forms and left contact details? Your policy!"

The woman held her hands up as if it was going to calm her down. "Correct. It was all a bit of a scene. The fire alarm went off, and we evacuated the building. Another child went missing, and within all the commotion, Miss Smythe got confused with protocol." Already the school was closing ranks together.

It was clearly Miss Smythe stood behind, now sobbing her heart out. "I'm so sorry," she managed. Gina couldn't even respond to her.

"What is the point of protocol, if no one adheres to it?" Gina pressed, her voice almost shouting.

The officers caught up then. "Okay, let's calm things down, shall we?"

From there they were taken into the office, where a couple of plump middle-aged women looked awkward, and quickly made themselves scarce.

They went over the details again, and again. There wasn't a lot more that could be gained. The bottom line was that someone had come and taken Lia right out from under the noses of the school.

One of the officers, the caretaker, and the deputy head were currently looking at the CCTV cameras for a clear shot, but it was useless. Nothing of any value could be found. Over an hour later and completely drained, Pops and Gina left to go home.

There was no sign of Lia.

The little girl was gone.

Chapter Thirty

The silence engulfed them both as they sat in the lounge. The television remained off. They didn't even bother to cut the atmosphere with the mundane. The emotions flowed high like electricity, and neither knew what to say to make the other feel any better.

She remembered Noah. The awful truth of why he didn't turn up for their date had then been overshadowed by the abduction of Lia. It was more than a coincidence.

Gina looked over at Pops and was about to speak when he held up his hand.

"What?" she said.

"It's not a good idea." He looked away. It was as if he could read her mind.

"What isn't?" she pressed but deep down she knew.

"Going out." He looked back at her, and gave a resigned smile. "You won't find her, and you cannot help everyone else."

"But what good does sitting here do?"

"It means people can find you when they find her."

"Do you think they'll find her?" she asked. Pops pulled himself stiffly out of his seat; he walked over to the table. He was shaking his head.

"No, I don't think anyone will find her."

Gina's eyes suddenly went wide. "What?"

He pointed to her laptop. "But you will."

"How do you know?"

He smiled again at her. "Because you and I are very similar."

She got up and made her way over to the screen, whilst he put on some coffee. Of late, or rather since his heart attack, they had become a lot closer. Not so much as in the love they shared, but something else. You couldn't label it, but Pops was aware of her. The *real* her. The things she could and couldn't do.

She pulled out her phone and searched for the name. She fired off a text and set to work on Google.

Within a few minutes her mobile went.

"Hey," she said. She was glad he'd called her.

"How're you doing?" Rogers said, his voice was filled with concern but had the professional edge that she had come to understand. Before she could respond he added, "Jesus, sorry. Such a stupid question! You feel like shit, right?"

She allowed a slight smile. He was a good man.

"I've been better."

"Look, we have nothing. I'm so sorry. I mean, we have a CCTV film of the guy, but honestly? It looks like every other guy. Everything is average, and yet this is something committed by someone who is anything but."

"Can I see it?"

Sweet Vigilante

There was a pause. He was mulling this over. He desperately wanted to help her, but he also wanted to keep his job.

"I'll see what I can do." Their conversation was deliberately brief. He had to be careful with how they communicated. Not everyone would understand the good Gina did, and fingers would be pointed at things like morals, and they could be accused of being lawless. That was why he always threatened that her position was under constant review.

At one time she'd asked, "Why?"

His response was quick and to the point. "You're not Batman, Gina."

He had a point.

"And Noah?" she asked. Lia's abduction had cast a shadow over him, but she still needed to know. The two had to be connected. There really couldn't be any other possibility. The chances of two apparently unrelated cases linking back to one person had odds so long they couldn't be calculated.

"Still searching CCTV. Not many are positioned around that area, and the ones that are have been vandalised. Hopefully we'll get something."

"Shit." It went quiet. Pops placed a black coffee in front of her.

"Oh, there was one thing. Obviously, this is classified information, but Noah had something written on his abdomen."

"His tummy?"

"Yes."

"What was it?"

"The word REJECTS."

Her heart skipped, and her stomach dropped to the floor. She knew. Man, did she know.

"Gina?" he said. "You there?"

"I'm here." But the words were prickly spikes and her throat was bone dry.

"That means something to you, doesn't it?"

"I have to go," she said and terminated the call. Rogers was left barking frustratedly into his handset, but there was no longer anybody on the other end.

Gina sat back in the chair and placed her hands on her head. She knew deep down. She couldn't explain it. Ever since she'd seen him on the television she knew he was out there hiding in the shadows like a sewer rat. He was skulking around, fitting into society with his business, and making it look like he was a great guy. She thought back to all of the times they'd almost got into a fight. They would both circle each other, sizing the other up, but something would stop them. They were two opposites allowing the other to live.

She couldn't explain it. She tried even lying to herself about it, but she could feel him. He was around. Watching.

"You found her?" Pops said looking hopeful.

"Not quite. But I know who took her." And that was only half the battle.

Sweet Vigilante

Chapter Thirty-One

Years ago

The sound of rain pounding down was never welcomed. For some reason the noise of it encouraged the adults to dish out more pain to the children, knowing that the sound of water hitting the roof masked any screams within. It was a ridiculous reason as there was no other house around for miles, and the road that ran outside the house barely had a handful of vehicles pass throughout the whole day.

As soon as the clouds gathered overhead and the sun shied away, the children cowered and found dark corners to hide in.

The new child had been ushered in. It stood with its head bowed down, snivelling in despair. It was a girl. Not very old. Left here to perish no doubt. Of all of the homes and all of the families she could've ended up with, she'd ended up here in hell.

She threw a glance back behind her just as the door was slammed shut. Gina already felt her own heart bleed. She could imagine the child waking up that morning thinking her day would be no more complicated than choosing cereal and sitting in front of cartoons. Some kind lies were probably uttered to fool the child unsuspectingly into the vehicle that brought her here. Then, only through the sudden absence of a parent, did the realisation hit her hard that she'd been tricked. Badly tricked. The worst trick that could ever be played on someone.

Gina's mind flashed back to a scenario not too dissimilar to how she came to be there herself. She still couldn't believe she hadn't seen it coming. Her mum had never been totally hands-on as a parent, but that didn't matter. She was there when Gina came home from school. Well, eventually. Sometimes other adults would come and look after her, but they were in a more supervisory capacity rather than to entertain. But through it all, Gina never once expected to be suddenly dumped out in the country with these people.

"Hey?" Gina said to the girl, but she got no response. "Come over here." But the child in front of her remained rigid and sobbing. It would get a lot worse for her before it got better.

"Ah, what?" Jeff said. "Look here, we got ourselves another weak one!"

"Leave her!" Gina said loudly but careful not to let the hatred out.

Jeff turned to her. "And what're you gonna do, huh?" He took a step closer, and Gina instantly straightened up and stepped back herself. "I remember your mum. She didn't even look at you for one last time. She was smiling too much about how she could now live her life!"

Gina went to say something but couldn't. She glanced around at some of the others. They all looked nervous. Eyes darting around unsure where to look. No one was happy here. How could they be? Things never got better no matter how much they closed their eyes and prayed to a god who had stopped listening to them.

"I'll deal with you later," Jeff said to her, grabbing at his crotch, and then laughing.

Gina felt sick. She hated the confrontation. She couldn't stand living here. The thought of him pawing at her made her sick. But the thought of him with the others was even worse.

When he was gone, a boy a year or so older than her placed a hand on her shoulder. "It'll be alright, Gina."

She smiled at him. They were in this together. Bound by abuse and neglect.

That was when the oldest lad scoffed. "The fuck you going to do?" He was Lewis, the golden boy. Adored by Jeff.

The boy ignored him. Sometimes it was best.

Lewis decided that it was time to take centre stage. To flex his muscles. He looked at them all with a scowl on his face. He hated them all—each and every one of them. He made that blatantly obvious. In his simple mind they were taking away the attention that should be on him.

"You stupid little shits!" he spat, looking at each one of them. Letting them know there was nowhere to hide. Any swift movement by him had them all flinching.

Jim Ody

"You think any of you are leaving here? You think you're going home?" He mocked them, he pretended to cry and then laughed hard, pointing at each one of them again. Innocent faces looked up at him, hope already draining.

"Nobody wants you, ya know! You are all rejects! That is all you'll ever be in life. In fact, that's what I will now call you. The Rejects!"

He then roared at them, not so much like a lion, but like a monster. He thrust forward and knocked a couple off of their feet. Gina lost balance, too.

Soon they were all huddled together in the corner, Lewis stood over them, at first spitting, and then chanting over and over again, "REJECTS! REJECTS!"

Jeff came back in and laughed along with him, and then joined in.

Then he grabbed Gina and dragged her away for her punishment. All through it, all she could hear was those words, "REJECTS, REJECTS!"

Chapter Thirty-Two

It didn't take Gina long on the search engine to find something. The web allowed you to find almost anything – in fact arguably you could find *anything*. You just needed to know where to look – search engines show you things that are readily available, but there are also ways to find anything that has ever been published, even if the page has been deleted or the website it was published on is no longer available or hosted. Everything leaves its own digital footprint. Look hard enough, and you will find it.

There were things going for Gina though. She knew Lewis and what he was like. He wasn't the type to hide; he needed to be in a position of power. Even if it was for a huge corporation, he would be at the top. He didn't like to answer to anyone. He had to bully his way through the day, taking enjoyment out of kicking the inconsequential folk below him.

His name and town brought up a number of stories. She clicked to the images option and there he was. Not once, not twice but all over the place. Each time smiling in a way that demanded that you worship him. He couldn't get enough of telling people how wonderful he was. It would always be his downfall.

With the mouse, she moved and clicked on pictures and links until she came to a webpage. Essentially, the business was construction. It looked like they bought up land and old buildings and made them into cheap housing or flats. In some cases, he was following on from what he had known as a child. He was providing a low standard of housing for those with nowhere else to go. Preying on the poor and needy.

She looked up the details of the business, hoping to find a telephone number. A way to track this rat down.

Everything was generic. It was all forms to fill in, and registered addresses that were out of town. In fact, out of the country. That didn't surprise her. It was fitting that his business venture was doing all it could to dodge taxes and, wherever possible the ability to be traced. It was also a subsidiary, owned by investors and financial companies. Web after sticky web of complexities to try and keep the authorities at bay.

"Just a thought, but why don't you try Facebook," Pops said, scrolling through the paper on his tablet. He recently made the move from physical to digital newspapers.

She looked at him first like he was an idiot, rolled her eyes and then slapped herself on the forehead. He was a clever old fool.

"Of course!" she said. Lewis wouldn't miss an opportunity to be on social media. He was bound to be on Twitter, if not Facebook.

One search and there he was.

Sweet Vigilante

She messaged him.

Where is she? Short and sweet.

She drew breath audibly, as she saw the flashing lines of an instant reply being written.

That took you a while. Call yourself a Superhero?

With anger she tapped back a response: ***I want her back. Unharmed. Now.***

"He's got her!" she said to Pops, who was now staring at her phone, his tablet now discarded on the table.

"You don't know that. Be careful."

And I want to be a billionaire. Lewis replied. He was enjoying himself.

You fucking idiot. You always were a bully. She went to send, but Pops held out his hand, and shook his head. She deleted it

What do you want?

Hmmm… He was teasing her now. This was everything he wanted. Cat and mouse. The hunt. The game. Him being in complete control.

Then he wrote: ***You know what I want.***

She looked over at Pops. He looked worried. He ran a bony hand through his thinning white hair. He no longer had the fight in him. He felt his age, and worse still, he felt too weak and old to protect her. He was less than immortal now.

Fine. Tell me where you are. First I want proof of Lia.

"What does he want?" Pops asked. His voice now shaking and his eyes filled with tears. He was tired to his core, and his joints ached. It was so frustrating getting old.

"He wants me, Pops. He wants me."

Jim Ody

Pops threw his hands up. "Wait. Let's think about this. How are you meant to get Lia safely back? He might kill you both!"

"He'll try."

"Gina, this is no time to act invincible. You're not! I'm not! Look at me?"

"I know. But our poor little girl!"

Pops patted her arm. It might've looked condescending had it been from someone else, but she knew he cared deeply about her. "I used to think I was a superhero. Honestly, I did. I was fit and strong. You know I did exactly what you do. I would go out and try to right the wrongs of the world, but d'you know what? You can't. It's not down to us. We have the police and the authorities. You should be passing this on to Rogers. He knows about these sorts of evil people. We can't take them on. You and I are fools to think we can. It's no longer about what is right, but egos."

"If I speak to Rogers, Lia dies."

Pops took a breath. "That is a possibility – but at least I'd still have you."

"But I saved her. I can't let her down."

"I know. I know."

And that was when the picture of Lia appeared. She looked scared, but she looked well.

Gina slipped over the picture in front of him. "I have to, Pops." The words came out slowly. "Look at this and tell me again not to go!" It wasn't fair and she knew it.

Where are you? She typed quickly.

I'm not going to tell you straight away. You'll have the police here. Go to the restaurant.

What restaurant?
Remember Noah? He added a laughing emoji.

She hesitated, and he added another line. *You've not asked me about him. How quickly you forget!!*

It was you. I know it was you.

You don't know anything!

Pops held up a hand again. "Don't get into any arguments with him."

"I know. It's…"

Pops got up. "Do what you have to do," he said. "You have my blessing. Just be careful." He knew she would, it was what he loved and disliked about her all at once. She was stubborn.

She nodded to him and then sent the final message.

I'm coming now.

Tell anyone, and you will both die.

I know. And she did. She'd seen the horrors that happened at his hands. He was given free reign to do whatever he wanted to do with the other children. Jeff encouraged him, somehow getting off on it.

Pops walked over and hugged her. "I know what you're gonna say, but do you want me to come too?"

She shook her head. "No, trust me on this one. I'm going to bring her home, Pops."

"I know you will." He said the words but he wasn't sure how much he believed them. This guy was unpredictable and crazy. Those two things were enough to worry the hell out of him.

Gina grabbed a few things then threw her arms around Pops.

"Take care," he said to her.

"I love you," she said.

"I love you, too."

Jim Ody

She smiled, glanced around the flat like it might be her last time, and then she left.

He watched the door close, and for no other reason than there was nothing else he could do he cried.

Chapter Thirty-Three

Gina was nervous as she walked up to the restaurant. She glanced all around but saw no one. A couple were walking hand in hand, oblivious to the rest of the world, and a lonely dog-walker made noises to the dog as it stopped and sniffed everywhere. The world was an interesting place to a dog. Normality flaunted itself at her, and she knew right then that it was what she wanted. She didn't need these added pressures.

Then her phone buzzed.

Go to the railway bridge where you used to work, whore.

She was shocked that he knew. It proved he had been following her all along; it also proved she didn't know.

Fine she replied. It was a bit of a walk but she was prepared for it. This was his game now, and she had to play by his rules. Like a counter-punching boxer, she risked being hit whilst holding back. But what choice did she have?

Jim Ody

She quickened her pace. She thought about jogging, but that would only bring attention to herself. She thought of Pops, and of Lynne. But mostly, she thought about her scared little girl waiting for her.

She passed the doorway she'd huddled in on her first day of begging. Then the alleyway where she'd performed a sexual act. This was all an area that held nothing but pain for her. She looked and saw only places she'd been kneeling down or bent over. Awful experiences from only a few days. She could only imagine what her life would've been like had she stayed out there.

This was all deliberate. He wanted her to see rock bottom again. He was forcing her to return there. Another act of control.

She followed the path down past the train tracks. Litter decorated the landscape, graffiti splashed colours over the walls. She was now in a place frequented only by vagrants and criminals. Even the railway workers refused to come to this part of the tracks to do repairs, despite the fence between themselves and the barren ground. But you didn't need to search far to find gaping holes in the fence. Every once in a while, someone got through, and then a team was sent to clear up the mess of body parts when they were sliced into pieces by a train.

She went down the embankment, below the tracks to where the deep dark bridge was. The resting place for many.

"Well, 'ello, babes!" a voice with a street accent, and a slight lisp said. He walked out wearing a grubby hoodie, behind him a couple of other lads grinned.

Sweet Vigilante

They looked rough, all missing teeth, and patchy facial hair. Products of a misspent youth.

"Leave now, and no one gets hurt," Gina said. She knew she could handle herself, but mostly that was against one person and often using the element of surprise. These three stood in front of her with nothing to lose. That made them incredibly dangerous.

"You's funny, init?" the guy said, grinning like a loon.

One of the others limped forward although it was hard to tell whether he was injured or thought this to be a macho swagger. His tracksuit bottoms seemed much too loose for him.

"Bitch, wanna 'ave fun, Fam, yeah?" They grinned and bumped fists.

"Seriously, I don't want to hurt anyone," Gina tried again.

"Babe's all hot, when she frontin', init?"

The leader walked forward in an exaggerated way, jigging his weight from foot to foot. He reached out to smooth her hair. In a quick move, she grabbed his wrist with one hand and smashed the palm of her hand as hard as she could on his now flat elbow. There was a sickening cracking sound as the momentum snapped the elbow the wrong way, popping it out. She swept away his legs from underneath him. With a dislocated elbow he was unable to cushion his fall.

She looked up as one of the others charged her. He was already pulling his fist back telling her in good time his intentions. As the huge and uncontrollable haymaker punch came flying over her, she ducked and slammed a one-two punch into his solar plexus, and kidneys. He went down. The other guy walked over with a bit more purpose. He was calm, and he was quick to go into a wide karate stance. He was either copying the movies, or he had some training. He could be dangerous.

They stood in front of each other. Circling around, with arms held high. One arm protecting the face, and the other ready to strike.

He jumped in with a jab, missed, but jumped back quickly out of range.

Gina tried her own jab, and it just glanced off his cheek as he turned his head.

He was better dressed. Not tall but without any fat on his body. He wore a T-shirt with a sport logo on it. His trainers looked new. He wasn't a down and out even if he was meant to look like one. He went for a back kick which caught her in the stomach. She'd moved slightly, but it still knocked some of the wind out of her. She feinted a body shot and threw an uppercut with her other hand. It made contact but only made him wobble. And hurt the twenty-seven bones in her hand like crazy.

He went for a wild swing and she jabbed him in the nose. The simple punch stunned him, and she took a half step back and kicked him hard against the side of his head. He went down.

It wasn't enough to stop him though. He flipped back to his feet and grinned at her. He was still confident; a little surprised, but looked like he enjoyed the challenge.

She looked up. Amongst the debris of cans and fag packets, a bar balanced on top of a ledge. It had been an area where some people had slept. Situated up high and with a view of all around, it was one of the safest places.

He came at her. He jabbed. One made contact, but she managed to move her head to the side for the next. She looked up again. He didn't know what she was doing.

He came again, but she moved. She looked like she was running, although she was circling away from his dominant right fist.

She held up her hand right as the bar fell down from above. In one move, she caught it and swung it hard at his head. He was too shocked to react, and with a sickening clang, he went down hard.

She turned to see the other guy make a half-hearted attempt to rush her. He screamed like a crazy person. She took a step to the side and swung a perfect back kick directly into his stomach. He went down hard, and instantly curled up hugging himself in pain.

She glanced over all three. The karate kid was out cold, and the others held their hands up in defeat.

"Okay, no more, yeah? We was just doin' what mans said, init."

"Choose your friends better," she sneered at them and walked off.

When she was at the other side of the bridge, she glanced back at the guys. The karate kid was moving now, and they were helping him to his feet. A few seconds later and they were all limping off in the opposite direction. She came out of the darkness, and looked at her phone.

Still alive? He added a laughing emoji.

Of course, she typed back. ***You might want to send an ambulance.***

Jim Ody

He responded first with a boxing glove and a grinning emoji, and then simply: ***Go to the old brewery in front of you.***

Are you brave enough to be there, or are you sending friends there too? She goaded. She wanted to add more, but could picture Pops waggling a finger of warning at her. Plus her face and hands hurt from fighting.

Those idiots are not my friends.* Of course. *I'm coming.

She had to hand it to him. Lewis had been clever in his thinking. Not only did it stop her being able to tell people where she was going, but he was in total control. He had made her walk a couple of miles, as well as fight three men. She was tired and worn out. Not to mention psychologically drained. He – on the other hand – was fresh and waiting for her. If it came down to it, he would have the upper hand - again.

The ground was hard underfoot. A mixture of rubble and hard mud. She was careful not to turn her ankle. Wouldn't that just be typical.

Gina walked up to the temporary fencing around the gutted building. She squeezed through a gap and looked up at the huge edifice looming over her.

She saw the mobile offices that made up the site office. From there she could see the main entrance. She looked all around aware just how alone and vulnerable she was.

She walked into the building.

A whiteboard featured scribbled instructions for her to go up to the third floor. She took the skeleton staircase up and around until she saw a door with a

Sweet Vigilante

huge number three on it. She opened it, and walked through. Her heart was pounding. Each second, she wondered whether it would be her last.

Another whiteboard told her to continue to the end. The scrawl in red pen seemed apt. She felt like a lab rat being coaxed into a trap. She did her best to second guess him, but what was it he wanted? Really, this couldn't be about sex? If it was, then maybe she had a chance. He wouldn't want to kill her until he'd got what he wanted. There lay her opportunity.

In front of her was a large door with a picture of Lia on it. Taunting her.

She quickened her steps and burst through.

A huge room opened out. It was an atrium showing floors above her. And over in the corner was a chair with someone tied up.

She walked over, but as she got closer, she realised it wasn't Lia. It was a man.

It was Abu.

Chapter Thirty-Four

Gina couldn't take it in. Her eyes were instantly drawn to the chair. The familiar person she knew so well. This arsehole was going for everyone she knew and loved.

She stopped and looked all around her expecting to see Lia or Pops, too. There was no one else. She turned back.

Slumped over in the chair, he looked out of it. She couldn't believe it. She wanted to grab her phone and make sure that Pops was alright. This bastard wanted to dominate her completely. Ever since she'd known him this was what he wanted. Total domination.

She walked forward, her steps slowing, not wanting to know whether Abu was anything but alright.

"And here she is!" A voice boomed from behind her.

She turned and Lewis stood looking incredibly proud of himself. He was tall and now broad and athletic. He wore an expensive looking suit and his

Sweet Vigilante

hair looked freshly trimmed. He'd become a handsome man, but of course he knew it all too well. She'd seen him on the television and also in pictures on the internet, but seeing him now in the flesh was surreal.

"What is it you want?" she said feeling defeated.

"You, of course. You have always been the thorn in my side. The little do-gooder. Helping out the other losers – the rejects – to wipe their arses and pull up their pants for them! You didn't help them, you just kept them being snivelling babies, *don't you see that?*"

"You abused them!"

"I was trying to harden them up!" he raged back. He was either being provocative or he actually believed it himself. "They were all abandoned. *You* were abandoned. They would've become stronger with me. I would've shown them that there is no love in this world. It's every man for himself! But instead, look at what you did. You kept them weak. And the weak die."

She couldn't believe him. Even now he tried to justify his actions. "You cannot blame me for what you did! You cannot change everyone to be emotionless. What did you expect them to be?"

He shook his head as he walked closer. "I'm an incredibly successful man, Gina. I have everything I want. Many, many people answer to me. What about you, huh? You work in a fucking book shop and live in a two-bedroom flat with a geriatric fool. Which of us would you say has done better?"

"That's not success!"

He laughed at her. "Oh please! Jealousy is a horrible trait. I'm a billionaire, you can only just pay your bills, and the rest of the rejects are dead. So, don't try and tell me that I made the wrong choices. Look in the mirror!" The last few words were spat out with anger. She got under his skin, probably in the same way he got under hers.

"You're a bully. Not to mention a murderer."

He pointed a finger at her. He was only a few feet away. "I am what life has made me." He smiled. There was something psychotic about him. "You're a fine one to talk about murder. You think you're so pure and innocent, huh? Who burns people alive? Tell me that!"

"Whoever did that deserves a medal. They deserved it. I just wish you'd been in that shed, too."

His eyes darted back and forth between hers. His mind was thinking fast. He was plotting and planning.

"It was you," he said, lowering his voice.

"That's a wild accusation. I was at the flat with Lia, Pops, and Lynne. Where were you?"

He smiled and nodded. "I see. Clever. Very clever."

Gina went to speak, but something told her to remain quiet. No one knew about it. She'd been completely in the clear. Really, despite the history, there was no real defence. She led three adults to a shed and set it on fire. A judge would take a dim view of that. Not to mention a good barrister could, and would, uncover her vigilante behaviour. That would show a huge disregard for the law and could be construed as her thinking herself to be above the law, and her own judge and jury. She would have supporters, but it wouldn't be enough to keep her out of prison.

No matter what happened, Lia would be abandoned again.

Sweet Vigilante

He narrowed his eyes at her. "You're very quiet all of a sudden? Cat got your tongue? Maybe you're not the angel you portray. Really, the sweet innocent superhero is just a monster!"

That enraged her. "No, you are the monster! I help people!"

He rolled his eyes. "Fuck off with that holier-than-thou shit, Gina. I don't want to help people. I want to make money. I want to take what is mine." His voice then took a sinister turn. "I want to kill you."

He pulled out a knife and thrust forward at her. She stepped to the side and tried to grab his wrist, but he turned and punched her in the stomach.

They parted and stood looking at each other.

"I know you can fight. I've seen you. But I can fight, too. I've trained. You think those three amateurs were any good? They are novices. You still took your time with them."

Gina managed to gain her breath again. "Overconfidence will kill a man," she said and spin-kicked him. She made contact, but he rode it well.

"Bravo!" he clapped in a mocking way. "You can't honestly think you can beat me though? You are just a woman, after all!"

She stared at the knife. It wobbled. His grip tightened, and he laughed.

"That won't work with me."

"Can't you see that, Gina? It's always been like this. We are opposites. You cannot hurt me. Your powers don't work with me."

A million things flashed through her mind. The instances when she'd been able to move objects. Not pick them up or make them float, it wasn't exactly

Jim Ody

telekinesis, but she could knock over or push things without touch. Unconsciously doing it. She'd assumed it to be coincidence. But now she was being told different. *Was this just another trick?*

"For your information, I've never wanted to have sex with you, Gina. That's not what all this has ever been about. I just want to kill you. I have powers, too, and you are the only person who stands in my way!"

That was all she could take.

She charged at him. Her punch landed on his nose, just as he swung the knife at her again. It sliced her hand. It wasn't deep, but it dripped blood.

"You need a knife to beat me though," she pointed out.

"I don't," he swung it at her, barely missing. "But I choose to."

"You know Jeff never wanted you there, don't you?" she said changing tack. "You got in the way. You were needy, always wanting to have sex with the girls. He called you a sissy, did you know that?"

"Shut up!" he spat. "He wanted me to be just like him!"

"But you weren't, were you? Jeff was hard each time with me. You couldn't perform though, could you?"

"That's not true."

"I was there, remember? You were like a kid trying to push marshmallows into a keyhole. Getting all cross with yourself. I saw Lyndsey laugh at you. That made it worse didn't it! She laid there and told you to man up!"

Sweet Vigilante

Lewis flashed with rage. He spun, kicked and as she was defending herself from the kick, he punched her full in the face. She went down. He jumped on her and stabbed her. Through pain, she moved her body to the right, but it was pulled out and sliced her again.

He punched her hard again. She felt the pain, and saw the flash of bright white light as she felt herself slip away. Unconsciousness pulled her out of reality, hugging her tightly and refusing to let go. Perhaps this was it. She'd blown it. Not just for herself but for Lia and Pops. For Lynne. For Baxter. For everyone in the future that she could help.

She wasn't aware of the gun going off. Even the huge sound that erupted and echoed around the building was lost on her body as it slipped away.

The room was a macabre scene. Abu bent over on a chair; Lewis laid down on the floor as blood spilled from his wound, and Gina unconscious in a discarded heap on the floor.

The man entered as quickly as his old legs would carry him, knowing again that he was too old for this.

"Gina?" He called wandering over to her.

"You old fool," Lewis said through quick breaths. "You should've stayed well clear!"

Pops looked at him and shook his head. "It seems to me that you're the fool," and trained the gun on him.

But he couldn't pull the trigger with the man laid there clearly in a bad way. When he'd first arrived, he'd seen Lewis attacking Gina. He didn't need to think about pulling the trigger, it was pure instinct, but now, what would he gain by killing him?

Jim Ody

"Gina?" he called again, ignoring Lewis whilst he checked on her. She was making noises which was a good sign. He tried to smile but couldn't.

"Abu," she muttered, and that was when another gun went off.

Pops dropped to the floor and grabbed his shoulder. He looked with surprise at the shooter.

The man who had been slumped over in the chair. Abu.

He stood up and stretched out his arms.

"So here we are," he said. "It all comes down to this."

"You've not changed, Abu," Pops said, clearly in pain.

"Abu?" Gina said, trying to come to her senses. She couldn't understand what was going on. She was confused; it was almost as if Abu had shot Pops.

He walked around them all, the barrel of the gun pointing at each. This was a side of Abu Gina had never seen. He was usually all about peace and love, meditation and reflection.

"What were you expecting? Did you not think I ever left my building?" He laughed at that.

Gina sat up. "But how are you involved in all this?" She found it all hard to take in.

"Look at him," Abu said, pointing to Lewis. "Tell me what you see."

And then it all clicked into place. The eyes. Both had the same dark eyes.

"He's your son?" she said in disbelief.

"Congratulations!" Even though he was holding the gun, he still clapped his hands.

"I don't understand?"

Abu shrugged like he didn't expect her to. "His mother was a whore. She ran off with some DJ when he was small. How was I going to look after him? I sent him away but kept in touch with him. D'you think he could make it on his own?"

"But?" Gina started. "What about Lia?"

"What about her?" He walked up and suddenly kicked her in the stomach.

"You don't think I could find another home? I have links to all of these places. Lewis knows what I'm like. You think I have people over for spiritual healing?" He chuckled at that. "Those kids didn't all die at the house. Some are still alive. Jeff made you think they died."

"Where are they? Where is Lia?" tears streamed down her face. Her stomach hurt – in fact throbbed. That was not the first blow she'd taken there today.

"Lia is fine. The others, not so much. I sold them. You'd be surprised just how much kids go for nowadays."

"You're an animal!" she screamed until the pain was too much. She stopped, as she coughed deeply.

Pops tried to move for his gun, but Abu was quicker. He kicked the gun away. It skidded well out of reach of anyone.

"Nice try!" Abu kicked out at Pops, but he grabbed the leg and spun on the floor knocking the man off of his feet. Abu swung the butt of the gun and connected with Pop's nose with a loud crack. Abu pulled himself to his feet, slightly embarrassed.

"You think you're a hero!" He scowled at them both. "You two think you're from some comic book.

Jim Ody

Bloody vigilantes. Just because you have nothing worthwhile in your lives."

He looked at Pops. "You allowed your woman to get her leg blown off. Big hero that day, huh?" He turned to Gina. "And you, you make a big play at rescuing that child, and then you allow her to be abducted again," he said, and tutted. "Shame on you!"

"You are a deluded man," Pops said, rubbing his face. Blood was now trickling down from a cut on the bridge of his nose. "You think you're a God. But a God of what? You are nothing!"

Abu placed the gun on the floor and kicked it over towards Lewis.

"Go on, son. Pick it up and shoot him. Then shoot her!"

Lewis slowly and painfully reached for the gun.

"You see," Abu said. "The fact that you always think you can save the day is your weakness. You should've called the police that day when your woman was in trouble, but no, you had to take care of things yourself. You almost died. She was the one who got shot and lost her leg, all because you couldn't take control and know when to call the police! Like now! You're a fool!"

Lewis picked up the gun and slowly moved it around.

"Shoot him, son."

Time stood still. Then a voice suddenly shouted from above. "Drop the weapon!"

Gina looked up and saw police in riot gear swarming in. More piled in behind them.

"It's over. Drop it now or we shoot!"

Sweet Vigilante

Lewis dropped the gun and slumped back.

"You see," said a voice amongst the police, and a woman with a limp appeared. "He didn't call the police because he thought you'd trace the call. But he did come and tell me, and I raised the alarm."

"Hands where I can see them!" One of the policemen shouted.

Abu laced his fingers behind his head and got down on his knees.

"I had his phone monitored," Abu said in frustration and shook his head. "But not yours. Looks like you saved the old bastard after all." And with that he moved one of his arms down quickly and into his jacket. Then there was a bang, a spray of blood, and the thud of his body hitting the ground. He went out the way Pops thought he would.

Of course, he had nothing inside his jacket. He just couldn't face the music. Not just this abduction but the evidence of the paedophile ring he was involved in. Not for his own pleasure, but as a business venture. His life in prison would be hard, but short. People like him were prone to fatal accidents.

Lewis was cuffed, and paramedics rushed to Pops and Gina. And through it all a beautiful sound rang out.

"Mummy!" a small voice cried. Lia ran through the crowd and towards Gina. Even though her ribs hurt like hell, and she leaked blood, Gina squeezed that child as tightly as she could. So much so that she saw black dots before her eyes.

Chapter Epilogue

Six months later

Pops had been in and out of hospital. His old body suffered from having the gunshot wound to his upper chest near his shoulder. The bullet had grazed the bone, which was painful enough, but the wound became infected. It damaged the muscle and took a lot out of him. When they thought it had all healed up, he developed pneumonia, and was back in hospital for a further three weeks. He was having a hard time. Sometimes men of his age don't get over it.

Even those that think of themselves as superheroes.

But Pops was stubborn enough to fight through it. He spent more time in his room, and as such invested in a huge television and computer setup. It was a sad sight that he was almost bedridden now, but he was determined to bring the entertainment to his room.

Sweet Vigilante

Some nights Lynne would sit in there whilst Pops used his nifty screen to help her research things for her books. They became a team. They became a couple.

Lia was resilient, and despite everything she'd been through, continued through life like it was all normal. Gina loved that about her, even if she did worry that when she hit her teens, everything would catch up with her and she would become overwhelmed by the things she refused to face now.

Gina had spent two long weeks in hospital. The stab wounds weren't deep, but she took a while to respond to the medication. When she was out, she worked hard at the bookshop in the day, and mostly she stayed in at night. Every once in a while, as Lia slept and Pops watched some American cop show, Gina would nod towards him, and with a resigned smile he'd nod back, she'd slip out into the night.

The world was still harbouring evil, and any help she could give the police made her feel better about herself.

She was always sure to tell Rogers exactly where she'd been and what she'd done.

Lewis was charged with abduction and multiple counts of attempted murder. It was an open and shut case. Or at least it would've been had it made it to court.

Lewis vanished whilst in police custody. Nobody could understand how it had happened. His cell was empty, and somehow he'd made it out of prison and disappeared into the shadows.

Then one night, Gina was sitting reading a horror novel, full engrossed. Everyone was asleep when her mobile rang making her jump out of her skin. She placed her book down and picked up her phone.

"Hello?" she said, wondering who would call at this hour.

A small frightened voice was at the other end of the phone. "Gina? Is that you? It's Tommy."

She couldn't believe it. The small child who she'd been forced to leave all those years ago was there, safe and at the end of the phone. His voice was deeper than the last time she'd heard it.

"Tommy!" she cried, her throat tightening up. "Little Tommy? Where are you?"

"I'm scared, Gina. They have my mum. They're going to kill her. Please help me!"

"Hold on, Tommy. Tell me where you are."

And he did.

Gina Chandler may not be an actual honest-to-God superhero with super powers. But she could be.

When she came off the phone, so began the next chapter of revenge, but that'll keep for another time.

The End

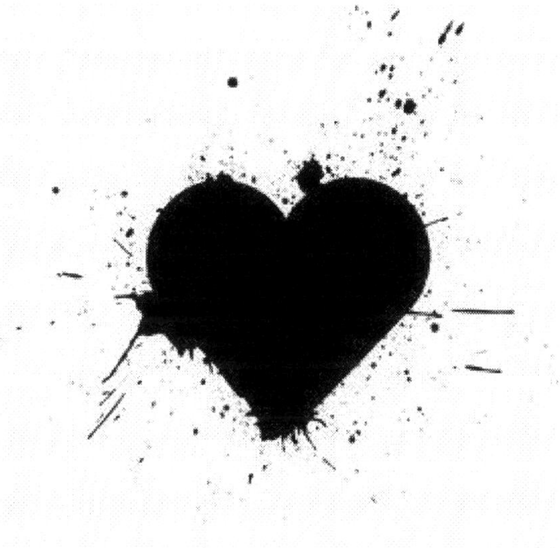

Acknowledgements

A big thank you to my family and friends. Your support is massive and continues to motivate me. This is a book that has been around for a while and I'm pleased it's finally with you.

Thanks to my BETA readers Sue & Andrea who didn't hate it.

A nod of appreciation to the hard work of my admin team: Zoé, Kate, Terry, Rosie, both Amandas and Ellie.

Thank you to Caroline, David and Jason for your continued support. Also, to Andy Barrett, Maggie James, Sarah Hardy, Valerie Dickenson, and Kerry Watts who also try to steer me in the right direction. Or try.

Thank you to Matt Rayner for your friendship, design and support with Question Mark Press. Everybody else at Question Mark Press: we are a great family!

A special mention to Elli Toney who not only designed the cover, but read the book and loved it enough to encourage me to get it released. Thank you so much!

And a huge thank you to Shelagh Corker for adding the final polish to my books.

I'll finish with a high-five, fist-bump, or hug (depending on current social distance rules) to you the reader. You are, and will always remain, incredibly special to me. The journey is far from over so sit back and enjoy the ride!

ABOUT THE AUTHOR

Jim writes dark Psychological/Thrillers, Horror and YA books that have endings you won't see coming, and favours stories packed with wit. He has written over a dozen novels and many more short-stories spanning many genres.

Jim has a very strange sense of humour and is often considered a little odd. When not writing he will be found playing the drums, watching football and eating chocolate. He lives with his long-suffering wife, three beautiful children and two indignant cats in Swindon, Wiltshire UK.

He is also the owner of Question Mark Press and enjoys helping new authors.

JIM ODY
Stories with a Twist

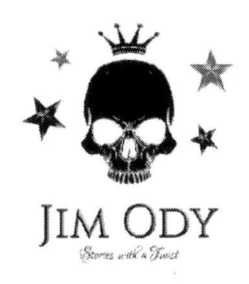

Connect with Jim Ody here:

Facebook: www.facebook.com/JimOdyAuthor
Jim Ody's Spooky Circus Street Team: https://www.facebook.com/groups/1372500609494122/
Amazon Author Link: https://www.amazon.co.uk/Jim-Ody/e/B019A6AMSY/
Email: jim.ody@hotmail.co.uk
Twitter: @Jim_Ody_Author
Instagram: @jimodyauthor
Pintrest: https://www.pinterest.co.uk/jimodyauthor/
Bookbub: https://www.bookbub.com/profile/jim-ody
www.questionmarkpress.com

Want to read more books by this author?

Here are details of three more books for you to get your hands on!

A Lifetime Ago (Hudson Bell Book1)

This is a tale about how the events of one day have such catastrophic consequences on the future.

Hudson Bell is a consultant for the police. A former DI, he spends his days helping to find missing children.

May and her son go on a road trip to celebrate his birthday; Robert and Nadia buy their dream house by the sea.

But as each look to enjoy a new life, none of them can shake off what happened on that fateful day. One of them blames the others and will stop at nothing to seek revenge.

One accident and five lives changed forever.

?

Question Mark Press

The Place That Never Existed

For Paul and Debbie it was meant to be the happiest time of their lives.

A small village wedding in front of their family and friends, followed by a quiet honeymoon in Devon. Not everyone had been happy to see them together. A woman from their past refused to accept it. Her actions over the previous year had ended in tragedy, and had almost broken the happy couple apart.

Now, away from it all in a picturesque log cabin, Paul and Debbie look forward to time spent alone together... But she has found out where they are, and she will stop at nothing to make sure that the marriage is over... forever.

But Huntswood Cove isn't just a beautiful Devonshire fishing town, it has its own secret. Recently, people have begun to disappear, only to turn up dead in suspicious circumstances. The locals begin to question what is going on. Soon everything strange points to the abandoned house in the woods.

The house that nobody wants to talk about. To them, it is the place that never existed.

?

Question Mark Press

The Crazy Season (Joel Baxter Book 1)

Joel Baxter is infamous for solving weird and bizarre cases that others avoid. So, when he receives an email from a teenage boy Tim saying his town is cursed, he cannot turn it down.

"...I will more than likely be dead when you read this. There is nothing I can do about it. It's the curse, and we've hit The Crazy Season." Every 20 years, there are a handful of unexplained teenage deaths and it's started again.

With the help of his straight-talking friend Melody, they set out to get to the bottom of the alleged curse. Everybody in Black Rock has secrets and nobody wants to speak.

The closer they get to truth the more Joel and Melody realise that their involvement is far from coincidental.

?

Question Mark Press

HAVE YOU GIVEN JIM ODY A TRY?

With 15 novels Jim is arguably a name among crime writing, known for shocking twists and nail biting standalones.

Check out his whole collection on Goodreads!

...and many more!

available at **amazon** kindle unlimited

2021 QUESTION MARK PRESS
NEW RELEASES

available at amazon

Stay tuned! More new releases this year coming soon...

Question Mark Horror

A new series of YA Horror books. One series by a handful of authors.

Are you ready?

1 – Camp Death
2 – Ouija

Question Mark Press

To find out more go to:
www.questionmarkpress.com